Power

By Cy Bishop

Power

The Endonshan Chronicles, Volume 3

Cy Bishop

Published by Cy Bishop, 2017.

POWER

First edition. June 17, 2017.

ISBN: 979-8227969170

Written by Cy Bishop.

With special thanks to God, my patient family, Google, and Jessica Dodson for the fantastic cover art.

'The Endonshan Chronicles' follows key
events in the historical timeline
of the planet Endonsha.
Each story is told from the perspective of
individuals best positioned to give the
clearest understanding of the event.
Book 1: DragonBond
Book 2: Sanaraheim
Book 3: Power
Book 4: Magic
Book 5: Invasion
Book 6: Traitors
Book 7: Feral

320 years before The Division

Chapter 1

With a pleasant afternoon sun gently filtering through the branches above and warming Mara's back, it could have been the perfect walk with her husband if it wasn't for the rough-looking group of thugs approaching from the opposite direction on the road.

She shifted closer to Mikell. His arm was tense; he'd probably spotted the men before she did. It wouldn't be an issue if they were still riding their friends' cart, but it had lost a wheel a few miles back. It was so close to Innsbrooke that they decided to walk the rest of the way. While they had traveled to the capital city several times over the last year to visit Kenara's ruler, Princess Tashan, this was the first time they had gotten an official royal invitation to dinner. They didn't want to wait on the wheel and risk being late. Perhaps that had been a poor choice.

Mikell adjusted his large pack and slid his arm around hers. The gesture probably looked fairly casual, but she knew how fast he could spin her away from danger if the situation called for it. She eyed the approaching group. Four men—no, five. Her husband was strong, but this would be too much. Better to avoid trouble entirely.

She brushed a wispy lock of nearly white-blond hair out of her eyes, using the gesture as a cover for her change in focus. She slowed her breathing as her eyes skimmed the group. Two Kadrians, two Nims, one Elf. The Kadrians and the darker-haired Nim were clearly not the leaders; they walked behind the others. The other Nim and the Elf both swaggered in front with equal confidence and control. Was it a shared leadership?

The Elf gave a subtle glance toward the Nim beside him. Checking for directions. The Nim was the leader.

Mara narrowed her focus on him, her face remaining impassive but her energy gathering inside her, swirling into a center point, ready to be unleashed.

Tashan had only taught her this trick on her last visit a couple months ago, and she hadn't mastered it yet.

"It has to be something they would naturally be thinking," the princess had said. "It's impossible to give them an idea or force them toward something they don't want to do. It's more like a little nudge, a breeze that tugs your shirt and makes it easier to lean one direction than the other. The decision will still be their own."

Mara kept her eyes on the leader's forehead. He undoubtedly had noticed Mikell pull her closer. She opened up a small stream of energy in his direction as she sent the message. *That man is protective. And well-armed. He might be trouble.*

The Nim seemed to be evaluating Mikell. Encouraged, Mara continued. *He looks like he knows what he's doing. And they don't seem to have much of value with them. It's not going to be worth the risk.*

They were only a handful of paces away. The leader now openly examined the two of them. He leaned closer to the Elf and said something too quiet to hear. If the trick had worked, it was directions to leave them alone. She could only hope.

"Hello, tabe," the Elf said to Mikell, over-enunciating the traditional Elf honorific. He evaluated Mara, his solid-colored charcoal eyes much darker than her own luminescent blue or her husband's deep brown. "Hello, raisa."

Mara tightened her grip on her husband's arm. Just a greeting to look inconspicuous as they passed? Or had she failed? The way the man had spoken the greetings made it sound like he wasn't used to traditional Elf society, but wanted to put on a show for their sake. It didn't necessarily give her any further clues to his motives; he could be trying to ingratiate himself to fellow Elves so they wouldn't think anything of their passing, or he could be trying to draw their attention to stop them.

Mikell gave a brusque nod. "Hello."

The group slowed to a stop. Mikell firmly brought Mara to a stop, then took one step further, placing himself between her and the men. Mara's heart alternated between fluttering over the hope that the men would move along without trouble and the sinking knowledge of the obvious: her trick had failed to dissuade the leader.

"Fine day for traveling," the Nim commented.

"Finer if we still had our conveyance," Mikell said. "Our friends had to stop to repair it. But I imagine they'll be catching up before long." With any hope, his suggestion of coming witnesses and possibly fighters would convince the group to leave them be. Mara watched the eyes of the men and saw no indication they had changed their minds.

"How unfortunate." The Nim glanced back at the other men, his high, sloping forehead barely wrinkled by his raised eyebrow. Their hands were on their weapons, ready.

"Enough," Mikell said, an irritated tone in his voice. He drew his sword. "Be on your way."

The men laughed. "I think you forget how outnumbered you are," the Nim said in a casual voice as his companions pulled out blades and clubs.

Mikell's hand nudged Mara to take another step backwards. "That's a matter of perspective. Move along. We have no interest in trouble."

The Kadrians exchanged glances. Mara eyed them. Perhaps she'd chosen the wrong target. She chose the smaller of the two, focusing between his pyramid-shaped ears which were positioned even higher on his head than normal for a Kadrian. *This guy is too confident to be bluffing. This isn't going to work. We should just leave.* Even if she didn't manage to get the group to move on, perhaps she could reduce their numbers by convincing some to run off.

The Nim snorted to show how unimpressed he was. "If you have no interest in trouble, then give us everything of value, and you and your lady may be on your way."

Mikell's muscles tightened at the sneer under the word 'lady.' Mara took another step backward without needing him to prod her. She trusted Mikell, but didn't like the way the Nim was goading him. Angry Mikell wasn't always as disciplined in his attacks as Calm Mikell, though he'd gotten much better since last year.

The leader drew his own sword and spun it in something that was probably meant to be an intimidating flourish, and might have been for someone else who didn't have the typical lanky, gangly legs of a Nim. "Last chance."

"Same to you," Mikell retorted, his stance lowering in preparation to fight.

Mara frantically tried to think of something she could say or do to stop this, to get the men to leave them alone. But it was too late. The Elf and the other Nim lunged forward, the Kadrians right behind them, as the leader stood back and smirked. Mikell deflected the first two strikes, dodged the third, blocked the fourth. The Elf was already darting back in for another attack. Mikell backed up a step and barely managed to block in time.

There were too many for Mikell to handle alone. Mara clenched her fists as she moved to maintain a safe distance from the fight without getting too far from Mikell's reach. She hated this, feeling helpless to do anything but watch. He'd taught her more after their adventure last year, more about how to defend herself and avoid danger, but that didn't help much here.

Mikell gave a brief glance back at her and sharply looked from her to the trees. He wanted her to run and hide. She instinctively turned to obey the direction. A good Elf wife allows her husband to fulfill his duty by protecting her.

But she couldn't just leave him. An idea popped into her head. She'd tried to make an attacker fall asleep last year, the way Tashan had, and managed to at least daze the man away from the attack. If she could just take one person out of the fight, it would improve the odds for Mikell. How could she not?

She cautiously circled around, cringing at every violent blow that her husband barely managed to parry or dodge. The men were moving too fast for her to get close. She'd end up getting hit and causing Mikell more trouble. The leader, on the other hand, still kept his distance. He wasn't too far from her. Maybe if she really focused, she could make him fall asleep. If their leader collapsed, the thugs would have to turn their attention away from Mikell, at least for a moment. She knew Mikell well enough to know that a moment was all he needed.

She watched for the right opening, and the instant the leader shifted his attention to the opposite side of the scuffle from her, she lunged for him. She planted a hand on his shoulder, focusing with every jolt of energy in her body. *Sleep. Sleep. Sleep!*

The leader blinked and looked at her in brief confusion. Before she could react, he grabbed her arm and yanked her against him. A dagger she didn't even see him draw flashed to her neck, the cold edge against her skin. "Stop," he barked.

The fighters backed off. Mikell panted, eying the men to make sure they weren't about to attack again, then spotted her. His light brown face turned a shade paler. Mara wanted to cry and scream and pass out all at once. She'd tried to help, and she'd only made things worse. She clutched at the man's hand, but it was solid against her. There would be no squirming away.

"Drop it," the leader said, the threat clear in his tone.

Mikell's countenance darkened. Mara tried to catch his eye, to tell him through her own eyes how sorry she was. He met her gaze, then subtly flicked a glance down to her neck.

She drew in a careful breath. He wanted her to do the thing he'd taught her shortly after their adventure. She wasn't certain she remembered it exactly. It wasn't like she had many opportunities to practice it. She moved her hands deliberately over her captor's grip, making it seem like she was still just grasping at him in fear. Her fingers found the right position. She looked to Mikell, ready.

"Let her go," Mikell said, his voice low and even, enough so to almost belie how furious and scared he was.

"I said, drop it," the leader repeated.

Mikell gave a tiny nod. Mara grabbed the man's thumb and yanked it with all her might, dragging his hand—and the knife—away from her. At the same time, she swung her other elbow into his side and threw her full weight toward the ground, angled away from him so she could roll and dash away.

She missed, landing in an ungraceful heap on the ground with a jarring shock through her shoulders. Fear blasted a fresh jolt of energy through her, and she scrambled to regain control, but only managed to scoot back a few paces. The leader would be able to grab her again, and—

But Mikell already stood in front of the leader, having moved at the same moment she acted, taking advantage of the distraction to dash past the others unimpeded. The tip of his blade rested at the leader's throat. The other attackers started forward, but the leader gestured them back without taking his eyes off Mikell.

"Tell them to move along," Mikell said, his voice better controlled now.

The Nim was silent for a moment before directing his men with a jerk of his head. The others put their weapons away and reluctantly turned back to their route along the road. Once they had gone a safe distance, Mikell stepped back and gestured for the leader to follow. The Nim smirked, gave a mocking bow to Mara, then ambled after his men.

Mikell watched for a moment longer, then grabbed Mara, pulled her to her feet, and raced into the forest. She was surprised how quickly it returned to her, dodging trees and roots at the fastest pace she could manage, as if it had been a month ago instead of a year that they had to flee in this manner.

A sharp pain had just developed in her side, making it hard to breathe, when Mikell finally slowed back down. He carefully checked the silent trees behind them before helping her sit on a large root. "What were you thinking?"

"I thought..." She panted. "I thought I could help."

He shook his head. "It's my job to keep you safe from harm. I can't do that if you put yourself in danger!"

She lowered her head, still fighting to catch her breath. Mikell was silent for a moment, then shrugged off the pack and handed her a waterskin. She drank deeply, and the pain in her side finally began to fade.

"You don't have any weapons, nor skill to use them," Mikell said. "What exactly did you think you were going to do to him?"

"I thought..." She avoided his eyes. "I thought I could make him fall asleep."

Mikell didn't answer. She took another drink of the water, regaining control over her breathing. He'd accepted that she could handle a lot more than he'd believed, and that her healing powers could do far more than either of them had known. Both of those facts had made themselves evident last year, when they'd helped rescue Princess Tashan. They'd endured days of running and hiding, fighting off attacks, and ultimately ending a war between Kenara and the Hranites in the neighboring land of Ebrun before it could even begin. The fact that she'd helped the princess repair the broken wall in seconds had made it impossible to ignore that she had strong magic within her.

It had been tense at first. Mikell had no love for magic users after what he'd been through, and with little wonder. He'd seen his village destroyed by a Hranite cult of magic users, joined the battle against them, and nearly lost his own life while witnessing untold horrors of the deadly force magic could be. But he'd changed over that journey as the princess's cousin, a magic-using Kadrian named Ari, helped him see that magic users could be noble, honorable people. The fact that his old comrade from the war against the cult, Korent, showed acceptance of magic users helped that process along, as well.

Still, it was hard to overcome the wounds of the past, though Mikell was in a far better state than he had been before their journey. Mostly he just ignored the new skills she'd been learning on their visits to Innsbrooke every few months and carried on as if nothing had changed. Moments like this, however, forced his attention onto her expanding skill set.

He straightened. "We should keep moving. They may still try to come after us." Back to ignoring. She was okay with that. He helped her up, looked her over, then pulled her into a tight embrace. "Raisa-me. I was afraid he would…"

"I'm sorry, tabe-me," she whispered.

He held her a moment longer, then took her hand and resumed the walk northward. They made their way through the trees for some distance before returning to the road. No sign of further waylayers, to Mara's relief, though traffic on the road increased as they drew nearer their nation's capital city.

Mara smiled as she saw the edges of the city ahead, the spire of the Meeting Hall protruding amongst the rooftops near the edge of the lake, and the shimmering palace secure on its island in the middle of the lake. The shimmer probably had more to do with the sun's reflection from the water, but it seemed fitting regardless.

They navigated the roads through the city with ease. Their frequent visits had made Innsbrooke almost like a second home, a dramatic change from the foreign city it had been to them when they first visited before their unintended ordeal last year. The original intent was to only visit once a year, twice at most, but Mara had quickly become consumed by the lessons Tashan gave her and the exploration of her abilities. Since a proper Elf husband is responsible for his wife's happiness, Mikell obligingly took her to Innsbrooke for more lessons whenever she desired.

The guards outside the Meeting Hall waved or nodded in greeting. Mara only remembered one of their names, Corret, a gangly Nim man. He saluted them and opened the door. As they passed, he leaned closer to Mikell. "Markur Rivon is in the Royal Room. Markur Kedlir is away for now, but you should find plenty of others happy to see you."

Mikell smiled. "Thank you, friend, but I have other plans today." The first time they came for a lesson, he had accompanied her to see the princess and stayed to rigidly watch, clearly uncomfortable. It hadn't taken much to convince him that she was plenty safe in the heavily-guarded Meeting Hall, and he'd ended up training and sparring with some of the guards who helped them last year. In their ensuing visits, he'd let her go alone to her lessons once they entered the Hall while he sought out his ever-growing group of friends amongst the guards.

The dinner invitation meant that today's visit took a different format. Instead of him going off to find guards and her seeking out the princess's meeting chamber, they walked together up the grand stairs and down a side hallway decorated with only a few austere touches, a tapestry on one side, a couple of portraits on the other. The simple elegance of the Hall's decor had made it easier for them to feel welcome in this foreign world of royalty and leadership, where they saw the princess regularly and occasionally crossed paths with some of the High Lords, though the members of the advisory council mostly kept to their meeting rooms on the west end of the building.

They reached the bedchamber they knew would be ready for them, settled their things, and got to work cleaning up and dressing for dinner. The long walk had gotten them to the Hall later than they intended.

"Do you think there will be a lot of people?" Mara asked as she combed her hair.

"I don't know." Mikell scowled at the formal belt he was making a poor attempt at tying. "I hope not. You're the one who's been spending all the time with her. Didn't she say anything about her plans?"

"No." Mara shooed his hands away and tied the belt properly. "Today makes a year, doesn't it? The best I can figure is she wanted to make some sort of commemoration."

"As long as she doesn't expect me to give a speech," he grunted.

They had just finished getting ready when one of the servants tapped on the door and led them to the princess's dining room. Mikell was visibly relieved to be in the smaller room instead of the massive Royal Room downstairs, where the grand feast had been held in celebration of their success last year. As opposed to the masses held in that room, the table here only seated eight at most. Tonight, the round surface was set for five.

Tashan already sat in one of the chairs. She stood and beamed, forming crinkles at the corners of her smooth, monolid eyes. "Mikell, Mara. I'm glad you were able to come on such short notice."

Mikell made a formal bow. Mara hurried past him and hugged her friend. "We're glad to come! It's good to see you again."

They sat, Mara beside Tashan and Mikell on Mara's other side. "How have the two of you been since your last visit?" Tashan asked.

"Well, thank you." Mara paused. "We did have some trouble on the road here."

Tashan raised an eyebrow. "What sort of trouble?"

"It was nothing," Mikell said, waving a hand dismissively.

"Waylayers," Mara said. "A group of five. They tried to rob us."

"Seeing how you both appear free of injury, I gather you were able to get away safely."

"Mikell was able to stop them." Mara gave her husband's hand a squeeze. He squeezed back, but only slightly. Clearly, he still wasn't happy about what happened.

"I'm glad for that. I'll speak with my guards about increasing patrols along the route. Thank you for bringing this to my attention."

"You know it's not your job to prevent every bad thing from happening. I don't believe it's even possible," Mara pointed out. The princess took too much responsibility on herself for her people's well-being.

"That may be the case." Tashan gave her a sideways grin. "But I can always try.".

"Are we expecting more?" Mikell asked, pointedly eyeing the two empty chairs.

"They should be here soon, I expect," Tashan said. "Kiven's cooking tonight, and Ari never turns down a meal from him."

Mara looked up, smiling. "Ari? We haven't seen her in a long time." She knew Ari stayed around Innsbrooke somewhere, but they hadn't come across her in any of their visits.

"She has a bad habit of keeping to herself."

"That's because whenever I venture out, certain people get me into trouble." Ari entered the room, Korent beside her.

"Korent!" Mikell greeted, his usually serious face breaking into a grin.

"Ari, it's good to see you," Mara said, then looked at Korent. "Both of you."

Korent nodded to them in greeting, then made an exaggerated bow to Tashan. "Milady."

Tashan laughed. "Come sit in your chair before I send it across the room after you."

Korent grinned, winked at Mara, and dropped into one of the empty chairs.

Ari slid into the other one. "What's this about? It must be important for you to send someone to track me down and deliver royal summons. I think I terrified your poor messenger."

"Terrified him?" Tashan asked with the amused expression of someone anticipating a story.

"I... may have mistaken him for an intruder."

"And she may have used a whip of water to hang him upside-down by his ankles." Korent's face reflected mock-innocence.

Ari rolled her eyes. "I put him down as soon as I saw who he was."

Tashan shook her head. "Remind me to give him a reward for dealing with the two of you."

The wording caught Mara's attention. She eyed Ari and Korent's hands and saw no marks of union. "Are you two..."

"I haven't quite convinced her of my better qualities yet," Korent said. Ari rolled her eyes. "But she has consented to regular visits," he continued.

"Because you kept showing up whether you were invited or not." Ari wore an annoyed look that was belied by the sparkle of amusement in her eyes.

Mikell cleared his throat. "We were also curious as to the intent of this dinner."

"I'm sure you are all aware that today marks one year since you bravely freed me and helped end Lord Mundin's plot against our land," Tashan began. The former High Lord had conspired with the Hranites to capture the princess and use her to gain land for the Hranites and power for Mundin. Mundin had been banished to Ebrun, where he undoubtedly met justice in the hands of the Hranites he had attempted to double-cross by declaring war instead of following the agreed-upon plan. "So today's dinner is in honor and celebration of you and your actions on my behalf, as well as on the behalf of all Kenara."

"But that's not the only reason," Ari said pointedly. "You'd be throwing a city-wide celebration if that was the case. Any excuse to hand out extra food to the citizens, right? Besides, you'd have Teylan and Losanna here, too."

"Yes, where are they?" Mara asked. "I saw Teylan a couple visits ago, but that was it." The burly Nim tavernkeep had been with them since they first discovered Princess Tashan was in danger, and Losanna, a powerful Tulvan, had joined them along the way and proved invaluable.

Tashan was smiling. "You're too astute, cousin. Losanna is escorting a group of High Lords to the Temple of Peace and will remain there for the traditional pilgrimage of her people. Teylan was recently married—"

"Married? Really?" Mara gasped in excitement. "Who?"

"Markur Kedlir," Mikell said. "Didn't I tell you he started spending time with her over the last year?"

"No, you didn't." Mara gave him a look. "You're supposed to tell me these things."

Mikell looked taken aback.

Korent chuckled. "You'll get used to being around women who speak their mind."

Mara blushed. It wasn't like her to correct her husband in public.

Ari elbowed Korent. "Quit embarrassing people. Tash, you were saying?"

Tashan continued, a slightly amused expression on her face. "Nim marriage traditions include a year away from work, so the two of them are travelling. Besides, I believe a smaller group will be ideal for this."

"Mm-hmm." Ari waggled a finger. "I knew you were up to something. What is 'this'?"

Tashan leaned back in her seat and regarded the four of them. "I must ask you to go on yet another adventure on my behalf."

Chapter 2

"I'm in," Korent declared.

"You don't even know what it is," Mikell said.

"Yup." The darker-toned Elf grinned at his former brother-at-arms, and Mikell rolled his eyes.

The food arrived, interrupting them momentarily. Once everyone's plates were overloaded with sumptuous foods and the servers had left, Tashan resumed. "You all know that Mundin used old writings about an ancient treasure to lure me to the Hranite trap. I've gathered information and studied my family's books over the last year, and I've confirmed what I had suspected the treasure might be."

"You didn't know?" Korent asked around a mouthful of food. Ari lightly swatted his arm.

"I suspected, but the writings were old and torn, with entire sections missing in some areas. With some more research, I found other writings and was able to piece together enough information to verify the matter." She leaned forward, eyes shining. "It's a gem, an uncut green stone the size of a person's head, and it can amplify a magic user's powers."

Mikell drew back, a frown on his face.

Ari's eyes widened. "Amplify?"

"Significantly amplify, at that. Can you imagine?" Tashan's face grew even more animated in excitement. "A healer enters a town ravaged by disease and heals every single person in an instant. A whirlwind tears its way through the land and is stopped by a single gesture. This could do so many amazing things to protect and help our people."

Ari's finger tapped against her chin, the vertical pupils in her green eyes sliding narrow. "That would be incredible. And it could wreak great devastation in the hands of someone with ill intent."

"Yes." Tashan sobered. "That's why it's vital this stone be found and secured. We don't know where the torn pages of writing ended up. I can't take the risk that someone else might find those pages and be led to the stone. Of course, I learned my lesson with our previous misadventure. It's unwise for me to pursue it myself. I need to send people I know I can trust, who I know for certain would never even be tempted to misuse this treasure."

"And that would be us," Korent translated unnecessarily.

"Yes." Tashan smiled at them. "I would hope that this journey will be far less dangerous than last year's, but I can't guarantee it. It's been over two centuries since the stone was hidden. I trust my ancestors found a place that would remain secure through the ages, but there's no telling what might be along the route now. I don't ask this as a command from your princess. I ask this as a favor for a friend, and you have every right to say no if you wish to abstain from further peril."

Korent shrugged. "I already said I'm in. I'm obligated now."

"Then I guess I better go along to keep you from getting yourself killed," Ari said.

Mikell looked at Mara, uncertainty on his face. She knew instinctively what direction his thoughts took. He was worried about putting her in danger again, and the idea that the stone increased magical abilities couldn't possibly sit well with him. She took his hand and leaned closer. "I'm willing to help. But if you don't wish to, we don't have to."

"You're not going to leave us without the second-best swordsmen in Kenara, are you?" Korent teased, earning another corrective nudge from Ari.

"You don't have to answer now," Tashan said. "I would rather you take time to weigh the implications than give a hasty response you might regret."

"What did your family's writings say about the danger?" Mikell asked.

"It would appear there's little. Granted, there may have been more information in the lost sections, but what I read seemed to indicate the stone was not so much protected as it was hidden, and hidden in such a way that it couldn't be merely stumbled upon by a random explorer. The pages give the impression it's hidden beneath a mountain, but there's little to indicate which one. There are several around the starting point, and even more within traveling distance."

Mikell nodded in thought. "What clues tell us where to go from this starting point?"

"None."

He looked up, startled.

Tashan shrugged. "The writings say that once you've found the starting point, the land will provide directions for those who know how to look."

"So we have little to tell us what to expect," Ari said.

"Correct." Tashan took a sip from her goblet. "With it being underground, my largest concerns would be the possibility that the cave system has collapsed in the time since the stone was hidden, and…" She glanced at them. "We know there are some beings that make their homes beneath the earth."

Mara felt a slight shudder. Most Kenarans, but especially the Elves, knew of the underdwellers, creatures living beneath the ground that could dig their way up and snatch you from the very dirt you stood on. "Did the writings say they're in that mountain?"

"They gave no indication, but even if they didn't at the time of writing, they might by now. It's impossible to say." Tashan looked at each of them in turn. "I know the weight of what I'm asking. As I said, none of you will be faulted if you choose to decline."

"Traveling for an unknown length of time to an unknown location with unknown dangers with no idea of how to locate what we're looking for?" Korent grinned. "What's to decline?"

Mikell simply returned his attention to his food.

"We'll provide you with whatever you might need for the journey," Tashan continued, addressing Ari and Korent without completely excluding Mara and Mikell. "I believe you will find the supplies more comfortable than last time. As well as the method of carrying them."

"What, no burlap sacks this time?" Korent joked.

Mara smiled. The journey last time hadn't been planned. They'd had to flee Innsbrooke when Mundin sent guards after them. Better supplies would certainly make the journey more comfortable.

Mikell sighed. "We'll go."

The note of reluctance in his voice might have caused someone else to check that he was certain, but Tashan only nodded with a smile. "I'm grateful for your willingness to help."

As the meal went on, they discussed further details of the plan. They would leave the next morning with a sentinal to speed their travel. That, and not having to hide from public eyes like last time, would certainly make the trip faster and easier. The conversation shifted to lighter subjects, catching up with each other's lives. By the time the servants brought dessert, they were reminiscing on their experience last year.

"Oh, no, it wasn't just a bump," Ari said, swinging her goblet in a wild gesture that somehow didn't slosh liquid everywhere. "He *tackled* me right off the edge of a ravine. We both went tumbling straight down into rocks, bushes, everything. I swear I still have bruises from that one."

Korent grinned sheepishly. "I don't believe I'll ever live that down. I confess, I have a weakness for leaping to action before I've quite thought everything through."

"Ah," Tashan said, taking another sip with an innocent expression. "That explains why you two make such a good match."

Ari made a face at her cousin while Korent and Mara laughed.

"Thank you again for your willingness to help," Tashan said as they finished. "I won't keep you up late. I'm sure you'll want your rest."

Mikell stood. "We do, thank you."

Mara wished the others a good night, then took her husband's arm and let him lead her back to their room. "You're certain you're all right with this, tabe-me?"

He undid the belt and dropped it on the floor, sighing as he relaxed without the constriction around his waist. "No. And yes. I'm not sure." He sat in a high-backed chair and pulled her onto his lap, holding her close. "It's dishonorable to deliberately take my raisa-me into danger. And it's dishonorable to refuse a request for help. And dishonorable to deny my ruler. And dishonorable to leave you abandoned for however long it takes to find this thing." He shook his head.

She ran her fingers through his dark hair, drawing her hands down the back of his neck in soothing strokes. Elf traditions were usually simple, but could easily become complicated, as in cases like this. "What do you want to do?"

A half-smile quirked his mouth. "I want to help the princess."

She kissed him. "Me, too. So we'll help the princess."

He chuckled and shook his head. "All right. We'll help the princess."

THE NEXT MORNING AFTER a hearty breakfast, they joined Ari and Korent in assessing and gathering the supplies. Tashan started out helping, but had to put Markur Rivon in charge of aiding them when one of the High Lords pulled her away with some questions.

"I'll be right back," she promised.

Ari waved her away. "Go. Be princess-y. We're fine here."

Mara did what she could to help but soon found her presence was unnecessary. She stood back and watched for a minute, then quietly excused herself. She wandered the familiar halls and soon found herself outside the princess's private meeting room. Was Tashan in there, or had the meeting taken place in the room for the High Lords? Mara didn't want to interrupt anything. But maybe Tashan was already done. Or perhaps the room was empty, and she could take a minute there to clear her head. It was worth checking. She cracked the door and peeked inside.

Princess Tashan sat in the middle of a large rug, surrounded by bits of paper and small objects. She looked up with a smile. "Mara. Come in, please."

"I didn't want to disrupt you," Mara said hesitantly.

"I could use a disruption." The Kadrian unfolded herself and minced her way free of the chaos around her, gesturing to it as she went. "We're beginning negotiations for the trade agreement with the Hranites. I've always found it easier to work out complex matters if I have some way of seeing all the factors involved. This one is becoming quite the headache, and I would enjoy an excuse to turn my mind elsewhere for a while." She inclined her head toward the hallway. "Care for one more lesson before you leave?"

"I'd love that." Mara smiled and fell in step beside the princess at a comfortable pace. Walking throughout their lessons had been established from the second session, and Mara found it made the process more interesting and enjoyable. They walked in silence for a few steps before Mara spoke again. "There's something I didn't tell you about the attack on the road yesterday. I tried to help. I tried to do the sleep trick again."

"You had only attempted that once before, yes? Last year, in the fight against the Hranites?"

"It didn't really work back then, but I was able to daze the attacker enough to help Mikell. After all I've learned from you, I thought for sure I could make it work right this time." Mara sighed and looked down. "It had no effect on him at all. I ended up causing more trouble for Mikell rather than helping."

"Drawing sleep over another person is one of the more complex undertakings. I apologize for my wording, but dazing the man in the fight last year likely had more to do with adrenaline and desperation rather than knowledge and ability."

"So how is it done? You've never taught me about it."

"I haven't, due to the complexity. You're a fast learner, Mara, and I'm pleased with how quickly you're progressing. I don't wish to give you something that will be more of a challenge than you're ready to take on." She gave another sideways grin. "Or are you finding my lessons too easy to master?"

Mara laughed. "Hardly. I attempted the redirect trick you showed me last time, and I still can't do it properly."

"That one is difficult even for the most experienced magic users. Simple in terms of energy usage, but tricky in terms of success. Don't measure your progress based on that." They reached a stairwell, and Tashan lightly ran her hand along the carved railing as they climbed. "When a person is excited, what happens?"

"Adrenaline, extra energy, extra attentiveness," Mara recited.

"And can a body be calmed while adrenaline still works through the system?"

"No."

They reached the top of the stairs. "To bring sleep upon another person is simple when the person is in a relaxed, calm state. Sleep itself is a healing process to the mind, so it only takes a gentle nudge to help it begin. Even one who struggles to fall asleep needs very little energy to overcome that obstacle and allow the process in."

"A healing nudge?" Mara had learned in their very first lesson that her energy usage differed based on what she was using it for, healing the body or connecting with the person, like in the redirection trick.

"Exactly." Tashan smiled. "But someone who is active and in a state of excitement is as far from sleep as possible. Thus, it requires several elements to activate simultaneously before sleep can occur. A connection is required to block the flow of adrenaline, and that has to be precise. At the same time, healing energy must bring a sense of calm, and then the final nudge to bring the sleep upon them."

Tashan raised an eyebrow as she continued. "I don't know if they told you, but when I used it on that guard last year, it took a few moments before he was asleep. It's not an instantaneous process. The sustained connection makes it that much more difficult."

"Block the adrenaline, healing for calm, and then nudge to sleep," Mara repeated.

"I want to be clear. Don't expect to be able to do this successfully until you have a couple more years of experience behind you, even as fast as you're learning." Tashan gave her a solemn look, fairly rare for the light-hearted princess. "Remember that a connection maintained has potential to go both ways. Don't attempt this until you've mastered the ability to control the connection and prevent the other person's energy from reaching you."

"So you're not going to teach me how to do it," Mara said.

"No." The gentle smile returned. "I will teach you everything that will be an adequate challenge for you to master, and we will progress upward from there. But drawing sleep is still a great distance above us. We'll reach it in time."

Mara nodded and continued walking at the princess's side for a few moments before speaking. "I only wish there was something I could do to help."

Tashan's eyebrow raised again. "Mending bone and flesh isn't helpful enough for you?"

"That's not what I mean." Mara couldn't help but smile at the ribbing tone. "In that fight on the road, Mikell was outnumbered. Healing isn't much help in a situation like that. I thought if I could put their leader to sleep, they would at least be distracted long enough for Mikell to gain the upper hand."

"I understand your frustration. You were afraid for your husband's safety, and you wish there was more you could do to help in moments like that."

Doubtful that was a situation Tashan ever found herself in, with her ability to reshape stone, draw the air into a whirlwind, or any of the other numerous magics she could control. It was rare for a magic user to be skilled in more than one area. Tashan, being skilled in all the magics, was all the more extraordinary.

Still, Mara appreciated the empathy. She looked ahead at the corner they approached without truly seeing the tapestry hanging on the wall directly in front of them. "Is there something that can be done as a healer? To attack?" The words stuck awkwardly inside her, but she pushed on. "To hurt someone?"

The solemn expression returned, with a darker tone now. There was a note of caution in Tashan's eyes before the princess returned her attention forward. Mara cringed internally. She'd obviously said the wrong thing. She knew it was terrible to consider using her magic to hurt someone else, but she hated standing by helplessly. She lowered her gaze and waited for Tashan to scold her for even thinking such a thing.

"How does healing work?" Tashan asked.

Mara nodded. Clearly the princess wanted to remind her of what a healer's true duty is. "Everyone has magic energy inside of them, but usually too little to actually use. That energy acts as a natural defense to protect the body from manipulation by magic users. The energy of a healer works together with the person's natural energy and is the only energy which can get past the defenses in order to heal." She sighed. "I know it isn't supposed to—"

"Is this energy spread equally throughout the body?"

Mara blinked, unsure about the direction this was going. "No. It's... centered primarily on the vital areas, though the less vital areas are still defended enough to prevent manipulation."

Tashan nodded. She was silent a moment longer. "The head, the neck, and the torso are strongly protected by that natural defense. But other areas, the extremities, aren't protected as strongly."

She stopped, and Mara did the same. The princess hovered a finger just above Mara's hand. "It's tricky. Dangerous. You have to send your energy into the hand as if healing. Then you blind the person's energy, lulling it into believing you are still healing while you draw your energy up—" she traced a line along Mara's arm, across the shoulder to the neck, and up to the base of the skull, "through their body and into the brain. The movement causes excruciating pain all the way. Once it reaches the brain, there is no going back. This energy was created to heal, not harm. Using it in this way causes irreparable damage to the victim. The extent of the damage depends on how long the energy remains within them."

The horror growing inside Mara at Tashan's description became too much. She flinched away, one hand instinctively rubbing at her shoulder where

Tashan's finger had drawn the path, as if doing so would erase the words from her mind. It took her a moment to find her voice. "That's terrible."

"It is."

Mara shook her head. "I could never do such a thing to a person. Anyone."

"Even if they were attacking your husband?"

Mara looked down the hallway, torn. "I... I don't know. No. Maybe. If he was in real trouble, perhaps." She shuddered. "Maybe just a little bit. The part that hurts in the arm and nothing more. I don't want to cause permanent damage."

The first trace of a smile returned. "You have a good heart." Tashan resumed walking.

Mara fell into step beside her, mind still working the matter through. "How do you convince someone's energy that you're healing when you're actually hurting?"

"You maintain a small healing touch within the person's hand and keep their energy focused there. It takes a great deal to accomplish. Like drawing sleep, this is still a great distance above us. Fortunately, very few know of this ability, and even fewer have the necessary power and skill to enact it."

A brush of relief passed through Mara's mind. She wasn't sure how she would have responded if Tashan had asked if she wanted to learn it that moment. She realized she was still rubbing her shoulder and forced herself to stop. "But there are some who can do it. How can it be stopped? How would I even know it's happening if someone near me was attacked this way?"

"You will see it on them as it happens. There's no mistaking it. As for how to stop it, you have to create a barrier within the path before the energy can get to the brain. Send in healing to a point along the path the energy hasn't reached yet, and consider it as an impenetrable wall. The attacker will have to stop there, making it impossible for them to maintain the connection."

Mara tried to wrap her mind around the instructions. "I don't understand. Can you show me?"

"Not without demonstrating the attack. And that can only be done on a person."

It took several more paces along their route before Mara gathered enough courage to voice her thought. "Then do it to me."

Tashan stopped and looked at her, one eyebrow quirked upward.

"I need to know what it looks like and how to stop it. Please."

The princess sighed. "It's agonizing."

Mara felt a sting of disappointment and bitterness. Tashan wasn't going to show her. Just like Mikell tried to shelter her from anything bad instead of trusting she could handle it.

"So you need to understand clearly that I won't do it for more than a moment, but it will feel much longer than that due to the pain," Tashan continued.

"Oh!" She should've known better. The princess never watered things down for her or held anything back. She braced herself. "Okay. I'm ready."

A faint sting hit her hand, spreading into an uncomfortably warm sensation along her wrist. Unpleasant, but not agonizing. Mara was about to say as much when her skin bulged out at the wrist as if a small creature had suddenly appeared beneath. Daggers of pain shot up her arm as the bulge flew upward, the creature burrowing its way through her skin, tearing and clawing and sending out runners of agony with each racing step.

Her throat burned from screams outside her control, her mind numb with terror and panic. Had to focus, a wall, a wall, how to make a wall? She blasted all of her energy at it, all she could muster. A warm sensation slid into her arm at the bicep, drawing her energy toward it, forming something solid and secure. The bulge hit the newly formed barrier and vanished along with the pain.

Mara gasped for air. She was sitting on the floor, unsure when that happened. Tashan sat cross-legged, waving some guards away before facing Mara and waiting. After a few more shaky breaths, Mara looked up at her teacher.

"You saw what it looked like?" Tashan asked.

Mara felt a fresh shudder ripple through her body. "Yes." It was all she could say for the moment.

Thankfully, Tashan didn't press for details. "You felt my energy form the wall?"

"Yes."

"You understand how it's done now?"

The way Tashan's energy had worked alongside her own showed her what she needed to know. "Yes."

Tashan nodded, satisfied. Then she paused and tilted her head in an almost teasing way. "I haven't put you off lessons forever now, have I?"

Mara managed a smile and even felt a tiny laugh slide free. "No." She took a deep breath, composure returning. "Not for a second."

"Good." Tashan stood and brushed off her skirt. "I believe that's adequate lessons for today, don't you? It's likely the others will be ready to leave soon. Though, as it happens, we're not far from the kitchen." She paused, a mock-serious look on her face. "There might be sweet-glazed hardrolls in need of liberation for the road ahead."

"We best look into that, then," Mara said, mirroring the expression. Then she grinned and followed the princess down the hallway, sneaking down a narrow stairwell to the kitchen's back entrance.

Mara was still licking sweet-glaze off her fingers when they returned to the others. Ari, Korent, and Mikell were loading a variety of items—food, water, ropes, torch oil and supplies, among others—into leather packs. Markur Rivon apparently was attending to something elsewhere now.

Mikell saw Mara's approach and left his packs to cross to her side. "I was about to send the guards to look for you. Markur Rivon is making sure the sentinal is saddled and ready. Once we have the supplies packed, we'll depart."

"Everything was satisfactory?" Tashan asked.

"More than, raisa-ro," he replied. "You have been most generous."

"It would hardly be proper to ask a favor and then fail to supply adequate provisions." She smiled, then continued over to Ari. "Are you sure you don't want to take the writings with you?"

Mara and Mikell helped finish packing the supplies as Ari answered. "I read them three times last night. If there were specific directions, they must have been in the missing passages. We'll just have to hope that your ancestors were right and something in the land will indicate how to find it."

"Our ancestors," Tashan said lightly. "You know my offer is still open."

Ari shook her head, but smiled. "You've given us all that you have for information, and you've given us plenty of supplies to work with, so we have all we need. Don't get yourself into too much trouble while we're not around to keep an eye on things."

"I make no promises." The princess grinned and hugged her cousin, then Mara, and Korent. She gave Mikell a polite bow. "Thank you again for being willing to help me with this. Maker's favor on all of you and your journey."

A flicker of excitement rippled through Mara as they walked out to the courtyard where a sentinal crouched, ready for them to board. The massive saddle on its back sat on a braced frame strapped to the animal, the riding section looking much like a larger, rounder version of the rafts the fishermen used at home, only with a short wall around the edges. She paused to relish the moment. Last year, they'd been thrown into their journey with no warning and had to flee for their lives. It was thrilling to get to look forward to the experience and leave at a more relaxed pace.

Markur Rivon saluted, then helped them climb aboard. "Safe travels. I don't know what she's asked of you, but I know there's no one I would trust more to accomplish her mission."

Mikell was the last to board, and he clasped hands with Rivon before climbing into the saddle. "Thank you, brother."

"Maker's favor. Come back with success and grand stories."

Mikell grinned. "I intend to."

Mara grinned, too, looking forward at the road ahead. It could be a simple walk through a mountain, or it could be a perilous journey with danger haunting their every step. Somehow, either possibility left her eager to find out what lay ahead.

Chapter 3

M*ikell*
Mikell sat beside his wife as Korent nudged the sentinal's neck. Everyone held on as the giant, lanky creature stood, air rushing around them strong enough to push them against the sidewalls of the massive saddle. It was over in moments, and he looked over the side at the city spread out far beneath them. Tiny people below skittered along the main road, weaving to the sides at each place the sentinal's long, avian feet planted in the middle of the street, and then back as the creature moved on. No doubt they were accustomed to seeing sentinals on the main road with regularity.

"What did she mean about her offer?" Mara asked Ari.

Ari waved a dismissive hand. "Something from our younger years. It's nothing. How have your lessons been going?"

The two women launched into a conversation about magic and Tashan's lessons as the sentinal left the city behind. Mikell adjusted his position and kept his focus on the road ahead. They would be confined to this saddle for about a day and a half. At least last time they had to travel in secret and remain fairly quiet. He didn't relish the next couple of days with nothing but chit-chat, especially with Ari.

Not to say he still looked at her the way he had when they first met. He'd thought she was insane and evil, corrupt throughout due to her immersion in magic. It was a perception that had been increasingly harder to hold onto as he saw her put herself in danger more than once to save others, Mara included. Ari was abrasive at times and had a temper, for sure, but she was fiercely loyal and dedicated to justice.

The real issue he had was the disturbing change in Mara. It was like he'd gone to Innsbrooke last year to celebrate his first-year sessen with his wife, Mara, and returned home to their village on the southern coast with... still Mara, but a different Mara. She had always been the epitome of Elf culture, quiet and thoughtful, polite and strong, intelligent and humble. She was his treasure, and she respected his highest duty to see to her protection.

The Mara who came back with him was mostly that, but somehow more outspoken, more independent, and—his greatest concern—more reckless, like what she'd done when they were attacked on the road. He didn't believe for a moment that Ari had nothing to do with that change.

Not to mention Mara's eager desire to learn more magic. He still had to regularly remind himself that magic on its own was not evil but was merely a tool, one that could be used for great deeds or terrible harm. He knew the latter all too well; he had only recently begun to see the former. And with no understanding of it himself, he had no way of knowing what it was Mara was learning and what impact it had on her. But he trusted the princess, which was the other thing he had to remind himself with every visit to Innsbrooke. Tashan would never teach Mara anything harmful.

"Are you awake?" Korent asked.

Mikell looked up, startled. "What?"

His friend chuckled. "I asked what you've done with yourself the last year. Other than losing your hearing."

Mikell gave Korent a look. "I was distracted." He returned his gaze to the road ahead. "Mostly the same as always, serving on the village guard. The biggest difference is the regular visits to Innsbrooke. I never used to be much for traveling." He leaned back. "I'm still not."

"So Mara's been learning from Tashan. I wasn't sure that would actually end up happening." Korent's attention remained forward, probably deliberate to avoid putting Mikell on the spot.

He appreciated the gesture, even as he was annoyed at the reference to his former attitude toward such things. "It's my duty to make certain she has what she needs and desires."

Korent's head bobbed in understanding. "And you're managing."

"I'm..." Mikell exhaled and looked down at the treetops below them. "It's fine. So. You and Ari?"

"Yup." Korent flashed a grin. "I think I'm wearing her down."

"A proper tabe respects a raisa's boundaries and accepts if she doesn't wish to be pursued." Mikell gave Korent a scolding look as he recited one of the cornerstone rules of manners in Elf culture. Even though his friend had been away from traditional Elf living for a long time now, it was surprising to see that he'd abandoned such foundational propriety.

Korent only laughed. "Relax your brow, snitface. Of course I would never push where I wasn't wanted. In fact, I did back off the first time she dismissed me. And then she asked me when I was going to start pursuing her again. Rules are a good place to start from, but every lady's desires are different. It's nice when you find one willing to provide directions."

Mikell found his gaze drifting back to Mara, who was giggling over something Ari had said. "Indeed." Mara was unafraid to be honest with him, but sometimes he knew he'd done something wrong without being entirely sure what it was. It would be so much easier if she would, as Korent put it, provide directions.

"Having some trouble?"

Yes. She's changed. I don't know what to do with that. He shrugged. "Isn't that the way of life?"

Korent looked at him a moment longer before turning his attention back to the road ahead. Mikell did the same. Not that either of them needed to; the sentinal was trained to remain on the main road. Besides, the wide-cut route was the only clear way for the creature to get through the dense forest with ease. With scarcely any need for sleep, their mount would walk through the night, get them as close to their destination as it could without leaving the road it had been trained to stay on, and then return alone to the palace while they set out on their mission.

Mara pulled Mikell into a conversation about changes in the village's defense strategies he'd implemented after their adventure last year, and the four of them chatted about similarly light subjects through the afternoon and into the evening. As the sun grew low and the first moon rose, Mikell gradually withdrew from the conversation. He'd wondered frequently on their previous journey if he'd made a mistake in choosing to help, but the threat to the princess's life had been too great for him to consider turning back. Now he wasn't sure what would keep him continuing onward.

He looked at Mara's lovely face as she laughed at something Ari had said, her pale eyes capturing the moonlight. She'd always been a foundation for him, the one who quieted his monsters and soothed his darkness. With the odd changes in her, it was like that foundation was crumbling. How could he be of any help to the others when he'd never felt so unsteady in his life?

Chapter 4

Mara listened to Ari and Korent speculating about potential dangers with only half an ear as it neared midday the next day. Mikell still seemed displeased. He'd mostly been quiet through their travels, talking occasionally with Korent and only rarely joining into conversation with the group as a whole.

She had a few guesses as to what was wrong—he was concerned about possible danger to her, he was displeased about the reminders of her magic use, Ari's presence reminded him too much of how vastly his core beliefs had been shattered—but she wasn't sure which one, or whether it was something else entirely.

"It shouldn't be much longer, right?" she asked.

Ari eyed the road below. They'd left the forest behind earlier that morning, and flat ground stretched toward a range of mountains leading south of the road. "We're not far."

"That's the mountain we vacationed under a year ago," Korent said, pointing to the nearest mountain.

"Oh!" Mara stared at it, but the rocky peak looked foreign from this high vantage. She leaned on the sidewall to peer down. The plains beneath them didn't look familiar, either, but they had been traveling a distance south of the main road last time. She looked that way only briefly; there wasn't much in the way of distinctive landmarks here. Round bushes and skinny trees dotted the plains with only the occasional area where they clustered together, each cluster indistinguishable from the others.

Korent slowed the sentinal before much longer, consulting briefly with Ari before bringing the creature to a full stop. It dutifully lowered its round body to the ground so they could dismount from the massive saddle.

Mara took a moment to lean over the sidewall to scratch the base of its neck as a means of thanking it before letting Mikell help her climb down the ladder to the ground below. Once they had all their bags in place, Korent patted the sentinal's leg. It stood and ambled along the main road back toward Innsbrooke, well trained to return to its home without needing the guidance of a rider.

"Which way?" Mikell asked. He scanned the area in all directions, always on close watch for potential threats. The main road was surprisingly empty in this long stretch between Emsha and Lifsi, the next main city along the route.

"South." Ari adjusted the bag on her back and started out, watching the sun closely to mark their location. Korent stayed close to her, and Mara stayed close to Mikell, wishing she could do or say something to ease the furrow in his brow that seemed to have taken up permanent residence.

Ari adjusted their aim a couple of times, and the new direction took them straight toward one of the larger clusters of bushes, shrubs, and thin, white lutri trees. Mara had to pull her cloak tight around her to keep it from being snagged on all the foliage. The thick bushes gave way to a vaguely oblong space of dense, long grass, then another mass of bushes.

"We couldn't have just gone around?" Mikell muttered as he pulled his sleeve free from a snag.

Ari pushed her way free of the cluster and came to an abrupt stop before anyone else was able to follow her out, her gaze scanning the sky. "No. This is it."

Korent turned around and pushed a twisted mass of branches and limbs aside so the others had as clear a path as possible. "In here?"

"Yes." Ari returned to the center of the space and looked around at the dense grass.

"No wonder Tashan and Alita were ambushed," Korent mused, examining the heavy cover of trees and bushes around them. "I think a herd of sentinals could surround this place without us ever noticing."

Mikell's brow furrow doubled as he took a slow look around the area.

Talk of ambushes wasn't comforting, nor was it necessary. "Thankfully, we aren't the targets of a Hranite plot," Mara said lightly, hoping to help his demeanor. "I doubt anyone even knows we're out here."

"So which way do we go?" Mikell asked.

Ari looked around. "I have no idea." Her tone was as light as Mara's, seemingly incongruous with her words.

"Well? What are we supposed to do, then?" Mikell demanded.

"The writings said the land will provide directions for those who know how to look," Ari said, walking to one of the lutri trees and examining its pale bark. "I suggest we start looking."

It was an effort to walk through the tall grass, and Mara was fairly certain she heard a hisser snake more than once, slowing her down and making her pay special attention to where she placed her feet. The reptiles wouldn't come after them if left alone, but with all the dense grass, it was hard to be sure she was giving them a respectful amount of space.

What made it even slower was that she didn't know what she was looking for. She checked through the grass, what rare patches of earth she could see, the trees, the bushes, and saw nothing out of the ordinary. Ari looked high into the lutris, examining every section of trunk and each branch for any signs of carved markers while Korent pushed his way through the dense mess of tangled bramblebucks snarled with leafy bristlaks, many of the bushes reaching high above his head. Mara wasn't entirely sure what Mikell was doing, but trusted that his pacing and muttering had something to do with searching for some clues as to what direction they should take.

"Any ideas?" Korent said after nearly an hour had passed.

"There's nothing here," Mikell grunted.

"I didn't find anything," Mara said.

Ari shook her head. "We need to find a different way of looking at this. Is there any pattern to how the plants are growing?"

"A pattern? In this chaos?" Mikell gestured with a snort, his hand almost getting tangled in a particularly thick mass of grass blades.

Korent studied the bushes. "Three bramblebucks and a bristlak, lutri, bristlak—no, that's the same bristlak—another bramblebuck, a wickernik, lutri, another wickernik, lutri, more wickerniks, bramblebuck..." He scanned the rest and shook his head. "There's no design or meaning here."

"How about the shape of the area? It's not a perfect circle," Mara offered.

They examined one end of the oval, then the other. If the shape was meant to provide directions, there was no way to tell.

"So that's it?" Mikell said, scowling at a lutri branch hanging low over his head. "We came all the way out here, and there's no way to tell which way to go from here?"

"I'm not ready to give up yet," Ari said. "The people who hid this wouldn't have made it easy to find, but wouldn't have made it impossible, either." She turned slowly, examining the cluster once more. "It may simply be that 'how to look' was a common phrase with a specific meaning when the directions were written a couple hundred years ago, but has lost that meaning by now."

Mara brushed her fingers over the grass tips around her waist. "True, and this would have looked a lot different then, too."

The others stared at her. "Say that again," Korent said.

She stared back, unsure why the sudden attention. "I just meant that things change in time. Coasts widen or shrink, plants grow, mountains wear down. This whole area probably looked much different back when your ancestors hid the stone than it does now."

Ari closed her eyes with a self-deprecating smile. "Of course. How foolish of me not to think of that."

"Foolish of all of us," Korent said, poking at the grass. "How much do you suppose has grown since then?"

"A lot." The Kadrian studied the area once more. "We better get to work."

While she and Korent, being taller, worked on taming the overgrown shrubs, Mara helped Mikell by shooing away hisser snakes and holding stubborn bits of grass still so he could cut the mass back. Their progress was slowed as they ran into various rocks protruding from the ground, Mikell's blade occasionally sparking against one they hadn't seen through the greenery. As the grass cleared away, it soon became evident the rocks formed a broad, roughly circular shape at one end of the oval, with a single rock positioned in the center.

Ari sat on the freshly shorn grass at the other end of the space and wiped at her forehead with a grubby hand, eying the late afternoon sky through the trees. "If I could control fire any better, I'd have taken care of this much faster. And easier."

Mara sat down, glad for a moment to rest. Mikell handed her a waterskin before taking a swig from his own. "Hard work never killed anyone," he said.

"Perhaps, but I don't like taking chances." Korent sprawled beside Ari. "So what do you see, oh lady of wisdom?"

Ari's face took on a vaguely amused expression as she nodded toward the circle of rocks at the southern end of the clearing. "I would imagine those have something to do with it."

Korent tipped his head so he could see them without getting up. "Huh. Okay, so how does that tell us which direction to go?"

"We have to know how to look." Ari sounded more like she was speaking to herself than the others as she stood and walked into the middle of the circle, examining the rock in the middle before inspecting the others around her.

"I would assume the center rock marks a starting position, and the rocks around the circle point directions, like a compass," Korent said.

"But which one points to where we're supposed to go?" Mara asked. "Is one of them different than the others?"

"Not in any noticeable way." Ari walked a slow perimeter around the outside of the ring. "But there must be something."

Mara took it on herself to collect their bags to the side of the circle, out of the way, and dig out some food for them to eat while they worked it out. Korent stood, walked into the center of the circle, and sprawled once more next to the central rock, on his stomach this time so he could examine the circle around him. Ari and Mikell continued walking in opposing circles around the outer edge of the ring, keeping their musings to themselves and only pausing to accept some food and waterskins from Mara.

After eating, Mara took a lap around the rocks herself, but there were no distinguishing marks or characteristics she could see. She spotted a nice reddish-toned rock and sat beside it, careful to make sure she'd left enough room for Ari and Mikell to continue their circuits. Korent similarly seemed to give up before long, and he rolled to his back and watched the continuing march around the periphery.

Mikell crouched beside a rock similar in tone to the one Mara sat beside. Mara eyed it and looked for any others with the same coloring. Perhaps that was the key? But she didn't see any others. The one in front of her seemed just like several others at random places around the circle. They weren't as nice-looking as this one, but similar, and completely random. She tugged at some of the jagged-cut blades of grass.

Mikell resumed his walk and paused by her, first studying the rock beside her and then turning to her. "Do you need anything?"

She shook her head. "I wish I could help."

He glanced at the sky. The shortened bushes made it easier to gauge the sun's position from inside the cluster. The day had shifted into evening. "I get the feeling we may be stuck here for a time." He paused to examine the rock once more, then continued on.

Ari passed from the opposite direction a moment later, crouching and lightly poking at the reddish rock from a few different angles.

"See anything?" Mara asked hopefully, partially out of an eagerness to continue their mission and partly out of an eagerness to move on from this boredom.

"No." Ari sighed, ran her hand over the rock, and moved on to crouch and poke at the next one.

"Is there a reason that rock is getting so much attention?" Korent asked.

Mikell and Ari both looked up from the different rocks they were examining, questions in their eyes.

"Not those." The Elf tipped his head back to look upside-down in Mara's direction. "That one."

"What do you mean?" Mikell asked.

"You both keep pausing by that rock."

Ari and Mikell exchanged a skeptical look. "I keep stopping because Mara's there," Mikell said.

"And you?" Korent prodded Ari.

"I didn't realize I was paying any more attention to that one than the others." She pursed her lips and studied the rock. "It's a nice-looking rock, but there aren't any markings on it, or anything to the color or shape that would suggest it's what we're looking for."

Korent rolled to a crouch and examined the rock. "Nice-looking? It looks like all the others."

Ari and Mara both spoke at the same time. "No, this one's…" They looked at each other, surprised.

"Different," Ari finished with contemplation in her tone, and her gaze fixed on the rock. She strode back over and tipped a hand toward its surface. Mara sensed the movement of energy; Ari was doing something magic-related.

After a moment, Ari laughed. "How to look. Clever."

"What? What is it?" Mikell demanded, scowling first at the offending rock and then at her.

"It didn't mean we should look with our eyes. This rock has been imbued with magic energy. It's faded after all this time, but it's definitely there." Ari smiled at Mara. "Our energies were drawn to it without either of us realizing."

Korent got to his feet beside the center rock, aiming his arm and pointing finger toward the marked rock from where he stood. "So that would be our direction, yes? If this was a compass, that would be south-southeast."

"I believe you're right." Ari pushed a mass of red curls out of her face as she straightened. "Only one way to find out. I'll keep my energy open to watch for anything else with this same energy in it."

Mikell's furrow deepened again. "Keep your energy open? What's that supposed to mean?"

"It means she's going to keep her energy around her like a shield," Mara said. "That way, she'll know right away if there's any magic energy nearby."

He eyed her, looking displeased. Whether it was because she knew so much about magic or because she had spoken out of turn by answering a question addressed to someone else, she wasn't sure.

"Sounds good to me." Korent swung his bag on his back and reached for Ari's bag. She rolled her eyes and snatched it before he could. He only grinned in response.

Mikell and Mara took their bags and followed the other two in the direction the rock pointed them. Mara slid her hand into Mikell's and was rewarded with a light squeeze. Still, she knew it would be best if she backed off some. She'd forgotten how hard all this must be for him. Not only were they seeking an artifact that amplified magic, but it turned out the only way to find it was through magic. He'd come to a reluctant tolerance of magic largely by ignoring its presence, but this couldn't be easy for him to ignore. She folded her arm around his and leaned her head on his shoulder as they walked, feeling him relax as she did so.

They walked for nearly an hour before Ari slowed. "There's something here."

Mara looked around. Aside from a few patches of birrik ferns, their leafy fronds curling upward toward the sun, it was all the same knee-high grass they'd been wading through since they left the last cluster.

"Where?" Mikell asked.

Ari slowly took a few more steps forward, then to the left. She reached down near her feet. "There's another rock here with the same magic energy as the last one."

"Another circle, too?" Korent asked.

"One way to find out." Mikell set to work cutting the grass back. Korent quickly joined in, Mara and Ari helping where they could. Sure enough, they soon uncovered a broad, rough circle of rocks, just like in the previous cluster.

Korent stood in the center of the circle again. "Which one did you say?"

Mara's eyes went to a dusty rock with yellow hues swirling across its surface at the same moment Ari pointed to that very rock. She had to admit, it was somewhat unnerving to already know which rock had magic in it. Tashan hadn't taught her anything about her energy being drawn to other energy without her being aware of it. She still wasn't sure how exactly she knew that rock was the one or how to consciously distinguish between them the way Ari did.

They moved on without further discussion, following their new direction southeast. The next time Ari stopped by an imbued rock, the men went straight to work clearing back the foliage.

Mara pulled her cloak tighter and hoped they found their way into the right mountain before too much longer. As far as the distance between rock circles stretched, it seemed they would only be able to find three or four more before it became too dark to go any further. They had materials for a temporary shelter, but she'd rather not rest in such a wide open space. Who knew when a stray dufo might wander by, or a clutch of wild trongials?

The others seemed to feel the same, as their pace in the new direction—almost due east—was faster than before. Mikell kept Mara close and occasionally glanced at the steadily dimming sky.

"I think we've circled around the back end of our previous temporary shelter," Korent observed. Mara had a hard time telling; it seemed that one peak blended into another.

The next one was easier to clear, as the mountain soil no longer supported the lush grass of the plains. Once the circle was uncovered, Korent stepped back and frowned at the rock Ari pointed out, which directed them southwest. "Are you sure that's the one?"

"It is," Mara said, looking that direction. They'd been traveling some degree of east this whole time. It seemed odd to be directed west so abruptly.

"Perhaps those who hid it wanted to throw outsiders off the trail by backtracking," Ari suggested.

"True. Or the mountain terrain might require a less direct route," Korent said.

Mikell only shook his head. Mara saw the impatience in his eyes.

The next one came sooner, after a mere half hour of walking up a gradual incline. Only a few thick, dry shrubs had to be cleared away to find the rocks protruding from the soil, distinguishable only because they were larger than the rest in the rocky ground. Now they went south.

"I hope this doesn't turn out to be some crazy tree-snit run," Mikell said.

"But if so, you've gotten some good fresh air and exercise," Korent returned cheerfully.

Mikell scowled at him, then at the near-dark sky. "It won't be much longer before we have to make camp."

Mara eyed the rough terrain. Perhaps the wide open plain would have been a better, or at least a softer, place to rest.

Another half hour found the next ring, pointing east. The next one after that didn't appear until after the sun had just dipped beneath the horizon. "North," Ari determined once they'd identified the other rocks forming the circle. She looked around. "Should we stop here? It won't be long before it's fully dark, and we'll have to start using up our torches."

"It's not particularly defensible," Mikell said, eyeing the sloping ground rising on either side of them.

"Do we really need to see that much?" Korent gestured at her. "It's not like we're finding these by sight."

Mikell looked at Mara. She wasn't sure if it would be better to stop while they were at one of the directional rings or press on in hopes the next one wasn't too far. Or better yet, in hopes of finding their way into the mountain. "I can handle going a bit longer."

"Then let's at least go to the next one," Mikell said.

Mara bit back a few yawns as they continued, Korent and Mikell both lighting torches before long. The ground rose some, then dropped rapidly enough that they had to slow down and place each step carefully. The rest of the terrain rose around them, cutting off what little light remained in the sky so the only way they could see was by the two torches. Mara put one foot in front of the other, just following Ari and Korent ahead of her, and almost didn't realize they'd slowed further until she nearly bumped Korent.

"What is it?" Mikell asked.

Korent extended his torch further. Just ahead, the ground on one side of them dropped away to nothing, leaving only a narrow ledge with a steep cliff face on one side and a drop-off on the other. It was too dark to tell anything further than that, but it looked like the narrow ledge continued along the same steep angle downward.

"That can't be the way," Mikell said, scowling at the ledge.

"This is the direction we're supposed to go," Ari said. "I can't imagine there would be a change without another circle to tell us which way, so we have to assume we're to keep moving forward."

Korent nodded. "It's possible the walkway was broader when the route was made. As Mara so astutely noted, things change with time."

"And we're going to try to walk that in the dark?" Mikell pressed.

Ari stepped out onto the ledge. In the darkness, it must have appeared narrower than it actually was, because she stood with her feet shoulder-width apart and still had space on either side. "I think we'll be all right. Unless you want to backtrack and make camp by the last circle."

Mikell eyed Mara once more, displeasure battling concern on his face. He didn't want to go back, but he was worried about her. "I'll be fine," she said.

"I'm not sure." He eyed the ledge again.

She frowned. "I said I'll be fine. If Ari can walk on it without a problem, then I can, too."

He looked taken aback. "It's my job to make sure you're safe. That means I have to be careful about where I lead you."

"But you aren't leading me. We're following the directions to find the stone for the princess, remember?"

He looked at Korent, then back at her, that second furrow reappearing on his brow. "Raisa-me..." His voice was tight. "Perhaps we should discuss this privately."

"We can tie a rope between the four of us," Korent interjected. "If someone slips, there will be three others keeping them up."

"If necessary, but that will take longer," Ari said.

"Let's just go," Mara said, stepping onto the ledge behind Ari. She was barely two-thirds Ari's size, so she had much more room around her on the rock surface.

Ari hesitated, but turned and led on. Korent slipped past Mara to keep a torch close to the lead. Mikell took a minute before he caught up behind Mara. He didn't say anything to her.

She didn't blame him. She didn't know why she'd spoken so sharply. It had been irritating to hear him second-guessing her when she said she'd be all right on the ledge, but she didn't usually snap at mere annoyances. Usually she was much more patient, especially with him, even when she chafed under his hovering and overprotection. She finally slowed a bit to close the gap he'd left between them. "I'm sorry."

"I don't understand why you spoke to me like that," he said.

You wouldn't. The snide barb shot through her mind, and she shot it down just as fast. She herself didn't entirely understand her response, after all. "I was irritated that you second-guessed me after I already said it would be okay. But I shouldn't have spoken to you the way I did."

He was silent a moment longer. "It's my job to keep you safe." He sounded even more confounded now.

She exhaled. "I know. I'm sorry."

Another moment passed before his hand slid into hers. "I forgive you. Please try to understand—"

"I know." She nodded. "You're my guardian. You have to watch out for my well-being." She hoped her eye roll wasn't revealed in her tone.

The ledge gradually widened, and the angle softened until it was nearly level. Mara kept yawning as they trudged along. Perhaps they should have stopped for the night back at the last circle.

They slowed again, and she looked up to see nothing but rock wall a short distance ahead. The path had widened enough to nearly be as large as the saddle they rode in on. In the torchlight, Mara could make out two possible routes. To the left, the cliff face seemed to have relaxed away from them, making a high slope that could be climbed on all fours if necessary. To the right, the ledge path took a sharp turn and continued the route downward along the new rock wall in front of them.

Ari frowned at the path in front of her. She pointed at a brown rock near her foot. "I found one, but…"

Korent lowered his torch to better illuminate the broad space around them, where dozens of rocks protruded in no discernable pattern. The one Ari pointed to was almost squarely in the middle of them all. "Oh," he said.

Mara studied the rock Ari had identified. It seemed nice enough, but not quite as much as the other ones had been.

Mikell scowled at the mess of rocks. "So how are we supposed to tell the direction without a circle?"

"They must have left some indication," Korent said. "Perhaps there are others that match it in appearance?" He and Mikell walked around the area, keeping their torches low.

Mara studied the rock a moment longer, then wandered closer to the rock wall ahead and found her gaze drawn to a different rock. "Ari? Does this one have magic in it?"

Ari frowned as she approached, scrutinizing the rock. Her face relaxed into a small smile. "Of course. They marked the entire circle to distinguish which rocks are part of it and which aren't."

"Then how would we tell which one is the right direction, if they all have the magic?" Mikell asked.

Ari didn't answer, her gaze distant. Mara recognized the look of concentration a moment before a tingle of energy washed over her. Ari was expanding and strengthening her energy field. Rock after rock seemed to light up with pinprick flickers, and one all but blazed with sparkling light.

"There it is!" Mara gasped.

"Where?" Korent asked, frowning.

"Here." Ari tapped the shining rock, then looked up at the direction indicated by the circle. Mara frowned as she looked the same way. It was a slight right turn from their current path, but to go that exact direction, they would walk straight into the rock wall.

"Are you sure that's the right rock?" Mikell asked, still scanning the cluster around their feet.

"Well, of course," Mara said. "It's the shiniest one."

Korent looked at her with a blank expression. "The only things shining here are our torches. All I see are a bunch of rocks."

Mara opened her mouth, looked down at the rocks sparkling in a ring around her, then turned to Ari, hoping the more experienced magic user would have some answers.

"Your energy is..." Ari paused in thought, "*interpreting* what my energy is showing. Your mind doesn't have a way to physically process what your energy detects, so it translates the energy into visible form for you. You see a visible shine, like I do, because of your magic."

"So you really don't see anything?" Mara asked, befuddled, looking first at Korent and then Mikell.

"Nothing." Korent shook his head.

"I saw a small reflection of sorts, but that was just something in one of the rocks catching the torchlight." Mikell eyed the rocks with displeasure. "Which way does your magic say we should go?"

Ari and Mara pointed.

"Into the wall?" Korent asked. "That will take some magic indeed."

"Tashan manipulates rocks," Mikell said. "Is that a family trait that was used to create an opening when they hid the stone?"

"Possibly, but they would have had no way of knowing future generations would have the same talent. I doubt they would have made it so specific," Ari said.

"So what do we do now?" Mikell asked, a bite of frustration in his tone. "Walk through a wall?"

"We could always try," Korent said cheerfully, earning a withering look from Mikell.

"We might at least take a look." Ari walked toward the wall. Korent followed while Mikell glowered.

Mara slid her hand into Mikell's again. She could feel the tension in his muscles, and she rubbed her fingertips against his skin, feeling the warmth between them. She couldn't entirely blame him for this one—if they had done all this work only to come to a dead end, she'd be just as upset.

"It's here," Ari said, a hint of excitement lilting her voice.

"What?" Mikell raised his torch just as Korent seemed to vanish into the solid surface. Mara followed her husband's quick strides over to the place where Ari stood. It was only when they were almost at her side that they saw Korent's torchlight beaming through the craggy surface.

"An opening." Ari had to turn sideways to step into the narrow tunnel.

Mikell moved back a few steps, then forward again. "I wouldn't have seen this if you hadn't found it."

"I think that's the idea," Korent supplied. "If you're going to hide something, best to put it where it's unlikely to be found."

Mara started toward the tunnel, but Mikell held her back. "Is it safe?" he asked. "There isn't much space to maneuver. I'd hate to run into something along the way." His fingers tightened on Mara's as he spoke, and she gently squeezed back. Last year, they'd accidentally sheltered in a dufo cave, and she'd nearly died in the ensuing fight. It was no surprise that he felt the need for special caution here.

Ari squinted at the route ahead. "Mara, do you know how to check and see if there's anything alive ahead?"

"Yes." It had been one of the princess's first lessons. Mara focused her energy toward the narrow opening and let it flow forward, breezing through the tunnel, and trusted that she'd sense if it came across anything living. She finally turned back to Ari. "There's nothing there."

Ari lifted a hand, the distant focused look on her face again. A slip of flame split off Korent's torch and floated ahead, dimly lighting the route. The tunnel climbed shortly, then levelled out and seemed to widen. The light stopped, nothing but darkness ahead.

"A cave entrance?" Korent asked.

"It looks like." Ari dropped her hand, and the light ahead vanished. "It's not far, so it won't hurt to take a look."

"Depending on what's in the cave," Mikell muttered, but he followed the others into the tunnel, leading Mara behind him this time.

The tunnel widened shortly, one side gradually leaning away so that they were walking on a ledge with a narrow crevasse on one side and a broad overhang above. The dark area ahead was indeed a cave entrance, opening up to a broad path into the mountain.

"Looks like we found it." Korent sounded pleased, relieved, and tired all at once.

"This should be a decent place to rest," Ari said.

Mikell raised his torch and walked into the cave for a distance, then returned, apparently satisfied there were no immediate threats. "I'll keep the first watch."

Korent eyed the narrow tunnel that had led to the area, then the overhang sheltering the path from above and the deep crevasse alongside. "It's unlikely anyone would stumble this way by accident. Your ancestors chose their hiding place well."

"Tashan's cleverness had to come from somewhere," Ari said with a shrug as she settled down to rest. "Let's get some sleep and start as early as possible tomorrow."

Mara dug into her pack for her blankets, then saw Mikell's puzzled look. It took her a moment to remember that he usually prepared her sleeping space for her. It was a husband's honor to see to his wife's every comfort, after all. "Sorry," she whispered, pressing the blankets into his hands and sitting back.

"It's nothing to apologize for." He still looked confused and bothered. He finished and turned to her as if about to say something, but shook his head instead. "Sleep well."

"You, too." Odd that she would have forgotten to leave it to him. It just felt natural to take care of things herself. She dismissed the thoughts and turned her focus to sleep. The next day, the real adventure would begin.

Chapter 5

M*ikell*
Mikell woke early and sat up, listening.

"Something wrong?" Korent whispered from where he leaned against the rock wall beside them, maintaining the watch.

Mikell listened a moment longer, then shook his head. "It's too quiet here. It's disconcerting."

"I think we're far removed from any other living being." Korent yawned and stretched. "Nothing else would be crazy enough to come this far out."

Mikell turned his attention to preparing breakfast. Korent joined him, and soon they had food ready for all four of them.

Mara stirred as Mikell brought her food over. "Morning already?" she mumbled.

"You can rest longer if you want." Part of him rebelled against the offer—*no, we need to set out so we can find this thing and get back home*—but after yesterday, he wanted to make extra certain he was adhering to his proper role as husband and guardian. If she needed more rest, she would have more rest.

"No, I'm fine." She sat up, making a futile gesture to smooth down her sleep-kinked hair, and took the food with a smile of thanks. Mikell smiled back, then sat beside her to dig into his own portion. Ari sat next to Korent, wrapping a leather cord around her thick mass of red curls before eating.

"What d'you suppose we'll find in there?" Korent asked around a mouthful of dried fruit, jerking a thumb toward the gaping cave.

"With any hope, the green stone we're looking for," Ari said.

He snorted. "I mean other than that."

Ari shrugged. "What does one typically find inside a mountain?"

"Rocks," Korent supplied.

"Do you think your ancestors would have left any traps along the way?" Mikell asked. They would need to be prepared for anything, since the writings left no clues as to what they would find.

It took Ari a moment to answer. "I think," she said carefully, "that the people who hid it most likely relied on the near-inaccessible hiding place as the main form of protection."

"Main form," Mikell echoed. "So there could be secondary measures to protect it."

"It's possible, I suppose." She shrugged again. "We don't know what was written on the parts that were missing. But I believe continuing as we have been—with me keeping my energy open—will get us through the best route."

"Could I help with that?" Mara asked.

Mikell felt like he'd just eaten a bitterroot whole, though he tried to keep his face neutral.

Ari glanced at him, then her. "If you wish. Though it likely would take more out of you than it does out of me, given our differences in experience."

"I don't want you wearing yourself out." Mikell gently touched his wife's arm, hoping she saw that he was only speaking out of concern. He'd seen how exhausted Mara became when she tried to do new things with her magic.

Mara's eyes flashed with an outrage so sharp he could barely breathe for a moment. But she blinked and looked away, taking a couple of deep breaths. "Okay. I understand." Her voice was still tight despite the acceptance in her words.

He stared, unsure how to respond. She'd never been like this before. She'd always been understanding, more so than anyone else he'd ever met. What had changed? He found his focus on Ari, thoughts and half-formed accusations crashing through his mind.

"I'm sure it'll be fine," Korent said in an overly loud voice. "Ari doesn't miss much."

"You flatter me," the Kadrian said dryly. "Are we ready?"

"Born ready." Korent bounced to his feet.

They gathered their things, and Korent and Mikell lit torches once more. "I think it best we all have light this time," Ari said, handing Mara a lit torch and igniting one for herself. The light flickered over Mara's fascinated expression, her gaze dancing across the dark cave entrance, their meager torchlights barely penetrating the depths.

Mikell kept his eyes on her as they proceeded. He'd already seen the massive cavern they were entering, with its top so high that torchlight wasn't adequate to reach it, the narrow ends of stalactites dripping down from nothing but darkness above. He stepped around a matching stalagmite, only paying enough attention to the choppy surface of the cave floor to keep from falling over himself.

Last year, Mara had approached their task with uncertainty but determination. Unsurprising, as she had little experience with running for her life or hiding from people seeking to kill her prior to then. He had seen she was more confident after their journey, but the contrast had never been thrown into such sharp relief as it was now. Instead of staying close to him and watching their surroundings with trepidation, Mara skipped ahead, turning around and taking in the cave with wonder. It was as if she was eager, perhaps even excited, to be on this journey. He knew she had changed some after last year, but now he was staring at a stranger.

Ari wove around one of the stalagmites, taking a slow walk through the cavern. Mikell took a few steps away, thinning out the light but illuminating more of the cavern to the left. Rock wall, more rock wall, and then a tunnel. "It's over here."

"Or here," Korent supplied, gesturing to a second tunnel.

"Or here," Ari said, lifting her torch to illuminate yet a third.

"Which is it?" Mara asked. She looked around at the ground, then paused. "Do you think they used the stalagmites to make one of the circles?"

"It's possible." Ari walked slowly around the protrusions near the tunnel she'd found, then wandered to Korent's.

"Well?" Mikell demanded.

"Nothing yet." She turned and walked back across the cavern to the tunnel near Mikell. It only took a moment before she smiled. "Here. It's this one."

"You found something?" Korent asked, joining them.

Ari rested her hand on a stalagmite just beside the tunnel entrance. "They made sure the correct route was clear enough, even without using a circle to point the way."

Mikell shifted his weight away from the stalagmite. "That one has the magic in it?"

"Yes. It's faint, but it's there."

Mara's hand slid into Mikell's free hand and gave a light squeeze. He felt the familiar warmth, a small comfort.

They continued through the tunnel. The surface sloped gradually downward, the torchlight casting odd shadows on the uneven walls that sometimes narrowed inward and then ballooned to create a wider path.

They had been walking nearly an hour when the wall to the right came to an abrupt end. Instead of a wall on that side, they now had a sharp drop-off into darkness, not too different from the long, narrow ledge they'd been on the night before. This one was wider, but a sheer cliff face stood to their left and nothing stood to their right. The only other difference was that the rock ceiling which formed the tunnel behind them continued along the route ahead, forming a broad overhang like the one they'd sheltered under.

Korent leaned toward the edge of the path, holding out his torch, but the light reached nothing, not above, not below, not anywhere around except the ledge beneath their feet, the wall to their left, and the wide outcropping above their heads. He whistled. "That's some cavern."

"How far down do you think it is?" Mara asked, stepping closer to the edge than Mikell liked. He tightened his grip on her hand.

Korent picked up a pebble and tossed it over the edge. They strained to listen in the silence.

A full minute passed before Mikell gently pulled Mara further away from the edge. "Too far. Are we sure this is the right way?"

"I haven't seen any other signs indicating we should change direction," Ari said. She tilted her head with slight amusement on her face. "Not that there were any other directions we could have gone once we entered the tunnel."

Mikell sighed. "We'll just have to be careful, then."

"This walkway is plenty wide. I'm sure we don't need to worry," Korent said, thumping his foot on the ground. He hit some loose rocks, and his foot slid sideways. Ari caught his arm before he could lose his balance. Korent brushed himself off, looking sheepish. "Careful. Right."

Mikell changed his hands around so his torch was in his right hand and Mara held his left, keeping himself between her and the drop-off. She looked vaguely amused, but only squeezed his hand without saying anything.

Thankfully, the floor that had narrowed and widened at random through the tunnel stayed more consistent in size here, giving them enough space to walk close to the wall with a healthy margin between them and the edge. Mikell kept his pace slower than normal, slowing further each time he felt his boots begin to slip on an uneven surface or a cluster of loose pebbles.

Ari stayed ahead of the group, showing the same confidence and sure-footedness as when Mikell first met her weaving through a riotous crowd. "Slow down a little," Korent said. "Let us slowmites keep up."

Ari glanced back with a teasing grin. "Having trouble?" She stepped, her foot landing closer to the edge margin. The rock cracked and gave way before she could react. Mara screamed as Korent and Mikell instinctively lunged forward. Ari caught herself on the side, one leg still on solid ground, and Korent helped her back up onto the ledge.

"Are you okay?" Mara asked, brushing past Mikell to crouch beside the Kadrian.

"I'm fine," Ari waved her off. She looked more embarrassed than hurt. She glanced up at Korent, matching his earlier sheepish expression. "Slower. Right."

He laughed as he helped her to her feet.

Mikell took Mara's hand once more, lowering his torch to get a closer look at the ground beneath them. He could see now the tiny fractures marking places where the surface beneath the edge had grown thin. "Stay close to the wall. The edge isn't stable enough to risk."

They moved on, this time walking much closer to each other to keep a larger space between themselves and the vast darkness to their right, and keeping their torches low enough to watch for dangerous patches in the path.

Ari stopped a distance further. "What is it?" Mikell asked, craning his neck to see around Korent and check the path ahead. The surface looked fine from what he could see.

Ari lifted her torch to illuminate the space above them instead. "That."

He hadn't realized the rock overhang had been gradually narrowing. Now there was only a small protrusion like a shelf above them, hardly more than a shoulderwidth. And now that the overhang had diminished, they could see a short way up the rock wall above them—and the large boulders that teetered precariously, kept from tumbling down the steep slope only by small outspurts and the narrow shelf above. Mikell immediately steered Mara tight against the wall, where there was still some protection from above.

"What do we do?" Korent kept his voice low.

"We keep going," Ari replied. "Very slowly. And quietly."

Mikell peered above as far as the light reached. With any hope, the collapse that sent these rocks from above had been limited and the space above them would clear up before long. "Stay close," he whispered to Mara as they cautiously proceeded. She nodded, keeping a tight grip on his hand.

The silence felt all the more oppressive with the threat of a rockslide literally hanging over their heads. Mikell kept alternating between staring at the rocks above them, watching for the first hint of movement, and watching the ledge ahead in hopes the danger would clear up soon.

Mara's feet hit a loose patch, and she caught his arm for balance with a startled yelp. Her eyes flew wide, and she slapped a hand over her mouth.

Mikell cringed and looked up at wobbling rocks above them. Korent and Ari remained frozen, watching same as he.

The wobble worsened. The rocks were going to fall.

"Run!" Mikell gripped Mara's hand and lunged forward, passing Korent as the other two turned to run with them. Torchlight flashed crazily around them, making the falling rocks seem to appear out of nowhere as they dodged and raced to get clear, Ari leading the group. Everything around them seemed to be shaking, even the very ground beneath their feet, making it hard to stay balanced.

Korent's shout was barely audible above the deafening roar of myriad rocks rushing down the slope. Mikell glanced back to see his friend tumbling as part of the ledge gave way. An extra shot of adrenaline raced through his veins. Get Mara to safety, go back for Korent.

But Mara's hand tore free from his. She darted back, catching Korent's arm and heaving backwards before he went over the edge. Korent caught the side of the ledge with his free arm and pulled himself the rest of the way up as a massive rock shot down the slope straight toward them.

"No!" Mikell leapt for them. He was too far away. He wouldn't reach them in time.

Korent lunged, knocking Mara and himself flat on the ledge. The rock flew over their heads.

Mikell ducked under another one smashing through too close to his head and scrambled forward. Ari leaned in beside him and helped pull the other two to their feet. "Go!" she shouted, pulling Korent onward. Mikell kept a tight grip around Mara's waist this time, almost carrying her the last of the distance. The shaking beneath them slowed as the slide diminished to just a light rush of remaining pebbles and grit.

It took a moment longer before they finally slowed to lean against the rock wall, panting for air and coughing at the clouds of dust the rockslide left behind. The oppressive silence was a relief now, signifying all was calm, the threat was over. Mikell clutched his knees, breathing around the pain in his side. When he finally had recovered his breath, the adrenaline still rushing through his system reasserted itself. "What were you thinking?" he demanded, spinning to face Mara. "You could have been killed! You nearly were!"

Mara stared at him from where she sat against the wall, shocked. "*Korent* could have been killed. What did you want me to do, watch him fall?"

"No! I expect you to get to safety so I can help him without having to worry about you!" He shook his head, glaring. His heart still pounded. All he could see in his mind was the image of that rock flying toward his beloved, over and over again. "What's wrong with you? How could you do that to me?"

Mara leapt to her feet, eyes flashing with sudden rage. If he hadn't known better, he would've thought he was looking at Ari's eyes during one of her fits of temper. "I'm not incompetent!" Her voice came out tight and measured. "I am not some fragile, glass-spun vase that you have to keep on a pedestal for fear of it breaking. I can help. I did help, for that matter. There's no reason for you to yell at me for saving our friend's life!"

Words failed Mikell between the shock at being spoken to that way and the fury clawing his insides apart. She was defending her actions? After she'd nearly been killed? "It's my job to—"

"Oh yes, do tell me about your *job*. I already know what your job is. I can barely even walk through the village without you hovering over my shoulder, certain something will leap out of the shadows and hurt me!"

He stared. "What's happened to you? Why are you acting like this?"

"Why am I acting like this? First you yell at me for trying to help you against those bandits, and now you're yelling at me for saving Korent's life! I think the question is, what's wrong with *you*?"

"Hey," Korent broke in. "She's right that she saved my life, brother. I think—"

"I don't care what you think," Mikell snapped.

"That's enough." Ari's voice held a sharp undernote of authority. "We're all safe. We're all alive. That's what matters. If you can't sort this out peaceably, then turn around and go back. This isn't helping anyone here."

"It's fine," Mara snipped before Mikell could respond. She stood, shouldered her bag, and walked up beside Ari. "Let's go."

The slope had loosed all it held, so they no longer had to watch above them, keeping their focus on watching for potential weak spots beneath their feet instead. Mikell aggressively kicked loose pebbles off the path as if clearing it, though he and Korent walked a distance behind Mara and Ari and there was no one else behind them to need a clear path. A roil of thoughts churned through him. How could she not understand that it was his most fundamental duty to keep her from harm, and that he couldn't fulfil that task if she threw herself headfirst into danger?

"She used to understand," he muttered after a while. Korent continued walking beside him without a word. "I don't know what happened to her. She used to never try to put herself into danger. And then she can't see why I'm upset that she could have gotten herself killed, can you believe it?"

Korent still didn't respond.

Mikell frowned. "You know I would have caught you as soon as Mara was safe."

"I'm sure you would have."

"And don't you agree that she's acting strangely?"

"I thought you didn't care what I think."

The words weren't pleasant to eat. He looked down and scuffed at a few more loose rocks. "I was angry. I shouldn't have said that."

"No, you shouldn't have." Korent shot him a sidelong glance. "But you're right. I noticed at the dinner she was speaking up more than she used to. I figured it was just that she's spent so much time with Tashan that she was comfortable to speak more freely, but as we've been traveling—you're right that she's changed." He took a few more steps in silence. "I don't necessarily agree with you that it's a change for the worse."

Mikell scowled. "She almost got herself killed."

"You just said yourself you'd have done the same."

"That's different." Mikell glanced ahead. He could tell by the tightness in Mara's walk that she was still mad. "Women are treasures. They're to be protected."

"She's a treasure, no question there. But I think she can handle more than you realize." Korent scratched the back of his neck. "Come to think of it, Ari's been a bit different, too."

"Different?" The Kadrian didn't seem to have changed that Mikell could see.

"She's been less impulsive. I mean, she's still impulsive, sure, just not as much as she used to be. And I haven't seen her lose her temper once. She still gets sharp when she's mad, but she doesn't yell like she used to. Or make it start raining." Korent grinned at the memory.

"Didn't you two say something about her hanging the messenger by his ankles?"

Korent gestured as if brushing the question aside. "It was late, growing dark, and she'd been having some trouble with thugs from upriver. Innsbrooke is clean and safe, but you don't have to go far into the forest before you start seeing trouble. It was an honest mistake."

"Huh." Mikell eyed Ari with suspicion, then Mara. Both had changed since last year. That couldn't be coincidental. It was looking like he was right; it was something to do with Ari that had created the change in his wife.

"I was impressed," Korent said after a moment. "You and I trained with full-grown men who didn't have fast enough reflexes to jump after me like Mara did."

Mikell managed a displeased grunt of acknowledgement.

"You can't tell me you aren't at least a little impressed."

Mikell shrugged.

Korent eyed him. "I get it, brother. You were scared you would lose her. Fear, panic, rocks flying all around—so we got to safety and you overreacted. It happens."

It took several more steps before Mikell could no longer fight off the truth he knew existed in those words. "I probably shouldn't have yelled like that."

"Probably nothing," Korent snorted. "It sure didn't help."

Mikell exhaled. "I'll apologize. But she needs to understand that she can't keep throwing herself in harm's way."

"Good luck with that conversation." Korent whistled lightly.

Mikell rolled his eyes at his friend, then turned his attention forward. The ladies had gotten a bit further ahead. His stomach mentioned that it was a good time to stop and eat a bit, and he decided that was a good idea. He and Korent would catch up to the ladies, they would all stop to eat, and he would pull Mara aside for a quiet, calm chat before they moved on.

A powerful cracking sound broke the air at the same moment the ledge under his feet vibrated. He braced himself, looking up for more falling rocks, ready to run ahead and pull Mara to safety. Mara and Ari had turned, similarly braced and searching for the danger. No falling rocks, so what—

The ledge shifted, and a whole chunk just behind them dropped away. Deep cracks like runners shot toward them. "Move!" Mikell bellowed, charging forward on shifting ground.

Mara bolted, to his relief. Ari looked back at Korent, then ran once she saw he was following. Cold terror intertwined with the adrenaline pulsing through Mikell's body. Even as he pushed harder and scrambled to dash over the solid parts of the ledge before they crumbled, he could see he wasn't going to make it.

The ground vanished from under them. Mikell lunged and barely caught an outspurt, his body slamming painfully into the rock wall. Cries echoed in his ears. Korent and Ari were gone. "No!" he shouted. Fear and pain pounded through his system.

"Mikell!" Mara cried. To his relief, the ledge beneath her was solid. Her torch lay on the ground, providing scant light as she lay beside it. She had one arm stretched outward as far as she could reach, straining toward him, but the distance between them was too great.

Another potent cracking sound. Mara gasped as the ledge beneath her shifted.

"Mara! Hold on!" Mikell yelled. His wife scrambled for a grip as the surface beneath her gave way, and she fell with a scream.

Mikell could only hear his heart pounding in his ears as he fought against the strain in his body, the agony of sharp rock digging into his fingers. He had to keep hold. He had to—

His fingers slipped, and then he was falling.

Chapter 6

Mara felt the groan through every last inch of her body. She cringed at the pain echoing back at her. Warmth instinctively spread to soothe the hurts. As she gained more awareness, she reigned it in, only allowing herself to heal the worst of the damage. She would conserve her energy until she had a better idea of the situation and how badly the others were hurt.

She tried to open her eyes several times before realizing that her eyes already were open. Her own frightened breathing filled the silent blackness around her. "Mikell?" Her voice was barely more than a whisper, but it still seemed too loud. There was no answer. "Ari? Korent?"

Nothing but silence.

Mara closed her eyes and took a deep breath. She had to keep herself together. Her pack was still on her back, and she pulled it off, wincing at myriad pains across her shoulders and arms triggered by the movement. She fumbled in the blackness, feeling for the opening, and came across a massive tear in the material. She felt the outsides of the pack. It couldn't have more than a quarter of what it had originally held.

After closing her eyes and taking another deep breath to maintain control of the rising panic, she reached through the torn opening and tried to feel out what was inside. Waterskin. Some rope. Food. Her fingers brushed a slightly greasy cloth covering a smooth wood shaft. A torch.

She pulled it out and wedged it on her lap. She didn't want to take any chances of it rolling away and disappearing into the dark. She only hoped her tinderlight wasn't one of the things that had been lost. She dug deeper and deeper, hoping and praying, until she finally found what she was looking for. She removed the tinderlight with a shaking hand and lit the torch.

The light blazed up so abruptly she had to scrunch her eyes shut at the painful flash. With a lot of squinting and blinking, her eyes finally adjusted, letting her see what was around her. She sat in a cramped space, made all the more cramped by dozens of caved-in rocks which likely accounted for most of her pains. She spotted one of her waterskins dangling between two rocks above her, and something that might have been one of her torches wedged even higher. But no one else was there. Her stomach twisted, and she looked up, trying to figure out where the others could be.

She didn't remember much of the fall, but it looked like she had tumbled into a narrow crevasse between two towering rock walls, one on each side. Behind her was the mountain of rocks. In front of her, the crevasse closed in on itself from the top down, leaving only a low tunnel that seemed to lead downward. That was the opposite way from where she wanted to go; she had to climb back up and find the others. If she had survived, then it was possible they had as well.

Mara took a moment to check her injuries and close a few cuts, then gathered up the bag as best as she could and started climbing up the cascade of fallen rocks, retrieving what few items she could find as she went. "Mikell? Can you hear me?" Her voice echoed back to her. Climbing was awkward with the torch in one hand, leaving only her fingertips free on that side, but she pushed on regardless.

A rock under her foot shifted, sending her sliding back down over the rough surface. She clenched her teeth and tried again, carefully placing each step, avoiding the rocks that wiggled too much. She craned her neck, trying to see higher. She still couldn't see the top edge of the crevasse. How far had she fallen?

The rocks rumbled and shifted under her weight. She squeaked and flattened against them, as if she could push them back into a semblance of stability. It failed. Rocks tumbled over each other as she hurried back down, rolling on top of some as she scrambled to stay ahead of this new slide. She reached the bottom and all but rolled into the low tunnel, flattening herself as much as possible against the side. Her torch flickered, the flame barely clinging to the oily rag in protest of the rough handling.

The rumbling finally stopped. A cloud of dust dried her throat and scratched her nose. She coughed and waved it clear, trying to similarly wave back the growing terror along with it. She was alone. She couldn't climb out. She had no idea where the others were. She didn't even know if the others were still alive. Her chest tightened. Why had she yelled at Mikell like that? He'd been unreasonable, but she should have been more patient. And now those angry words might be the last ones between them.

Tears bit her eyes. Part of her wanted to crawl back out and rush up the rockslide, even if it killed her. Another part just wanted to curl up and cry and never move again. She drew in a shaky breath as the hot tears slipped free.

A sense of distant presence shifted in the back corner of her mind. She sat upright, nearly banging her head. Ari was alive. Relief flooded through Mara. Mikell hadn't been far from Ari. If Ari was alive, then it was likely he was, too.

Mara felt suddenly foolish. She already knew a way to find people she'd been separated from. She couldn't believe she hadn't remembered to try it until now. Focusing on the image of her husband in her mind, she released her energy to locate him. It used to take a lot out of her, but now it was hardly more than a thought.

She felt the odd sensation of movement which normally would be paired with a dizzying visual of the ground rushing past. The blackness of the cavern made it impossible to see such a thing. She felt it stop without seeing anything but more darkness.

Frustrated, she smacked her free hand on the rock floor beside her. Of course she wouldn't be able to see it properly down here in the dark. The only thing she could tell was they were a bit higher than she was—or maybe a lot higher—and somewhere in the direction that was currently blocked by the rockslide. Still, she reminded herself, the fact that she'd been able to seek him out at all meant he was alive. There was still hope.

She gathered her bag once more, looked back at the rockslide, and turned to crawl down the low tunnel. She would have to follow this route until she could find her way back to him.

Chapter 7

M*ikell* The hum of distant voices buzzed around Mikell. They grew more distinct, one of them louder and more insistent. He cracked an eye and was rewarded by the sight of Korent's face in his own. "Back off," he mumbled, unsure if the words came out clearly.

"Well? You awake?" Korent poked Mikell's right shoulder repeatedly.

"I said, back off, munkbrain," Mikell grunted crossly, swatting Korent's finger away.

"He's fine," Korent said cheerfully as he straightened and moved out of Mikell's line of sight.

Mikell blinked while his surroundings swirled back into order. A single torch wedged between two rocks illuminated a rounded cave room, only a dozen paces across any direction. Behind him, rocks cascaded from a plugged opening. At the other end of the room, the ceiling dropped low enough they'd have to crawl to get under it. Part of the hum he'd heard was the flow of water forming a narrow river streaming through the far side of the space. Ari sat on a upspurt of rock beside the river, looking pale, and Korent gingerly climbed on the caved-in rocks, testing them. Both were dirty, scraped, and plenty bruised.

The first thing that occurred to Mikell was that there were no obvious exits from the room, save underwater through the river. The second was that Mara was missing.

He bolted upright, ignoring the pain shooting through his body. "Mara! Where is she? What happened?"

"She slid a different direction than we did. I don't know where she ended up." Ari leaned over her leg, and a thin slip of water flowed through the air to wrap around her ankle. "But I can tell you she's alive."

An ominous rumble filled the space as several of the rocks shifted beneath Korent. He quickly backed off and climbed back down. "It's too unstable. There's no way we can clear it without triggering another slide."

"What do you mean? How can you know she's alive if you don't know where she is?" Mikell demanded. He narrowed his eyes as his mind flicked through connections and possibilities. "You used that magic thing to find her, right? So you actually did see her? Wouldn't you know where she is, then?"

Korent brushed the grit off his hands. "I thought you couldn't do that trick."

"Of course she can. She taught Mara how to do it," Mikell said impatiently.

"I can't do it well. And it takes more energy than I have to spare at the moment."

Mikell eyed her drawn face. "Which means you did do something magic already. You weren't this exhausted before we fell. So what did you do, if it wasn't finding Mara? And how do you know Mara's alive? How can we find her?"

"Slow down." Korent frowned. "Let her take a breath, huh?"

Ari rubbed at her forehead in exhaustion, or perhaps exasperation. "Your first question—I created a blast of wind to cushion our fall. It's not something I'm very skilled with, which is why it took so much out of me. I believe it was enough to help Mara, as well, though it may have also pushed her further away from us. It's hard to say."

"Okay," Mikell prompted, folding his arms. "Now what about Mara?"

"I know she's alive the same way I knew Tashan was alive last year. We have a connection."

Mikell scowled. The changes in Mara, the uncharacteristic recklessness she'd been showing, the way her eyes had flashed in anger just like Ari's did—he'd been right to suspect it was all Ari's fault. "What did you do to her?" he demanded.

Ari looked taken aback. "It was nothing I did to her. When she and I helped Tashan raise the wall, we shared our energy in a way that amplified it, making it enough to do something none of us would have been strong enough to do on our own. That shared energy created the connection between us. I might not know where she is, but I can sense her. She's alive."

"That's why she's so reckless now," Mikell snapped. "Because of you and your connection with her."

"I would think you'd be more interested in the last thing she said. You know, the part where your wife is alive?" Korent pointed out.

Korent was right. Ari had to be telling the truth that the women were connected; it was the only way to explain Mara's change. Which meant Ari knew what she was talking about when she said Mara was alive. "Fine. How do we find her?"

"I think we need to find a way out of here first," Ari said. She reached for Korent to help her up, took half a step, and stumbled with a wince, favoring the leg she'd put the water on.

"Sit back down," Korent said, reaching to help her.

Ari shook her head and took a couple more halting steps, getting a decent limp going. "I'll manage." She glanced at Mikell. "We should take care of that gash."

"What gash?" He felt his left shoulder and found blood. No wonder that arm hurt so much.

Korent grabbed one of the two packs sitting beside the torch. The other one had a hole at the top and looked much emptier than it had been. Mikell peeled off his own pack, careful around the wound on his shoulder. It looked like it had survived the fall, barely. He inspected himself and the pack contents for damage while Korent cleaned and bandaged the shoulder wound. He was as thoroughly scraped and bruised as Ari and Korent, but it didn't look like he had anything else that needed tending beyond the shoulder.

Ari knelt beside the river, one hand in the water. Once he and Korent were done, she looked back at them. "I don't think we'll have to be underwater too long."

"You don't think?" Mikell frowned at the water. He didn't relish the idea of surviving the cave-in only to drown.

"It's easy to tell what's underwater. Not so easy to tell what's above it." Ari shrugged. "Not that we have a lot of choice. If it comes to it, there are things I can do to help."

"You have enough energy left for that?" Korent asked.

She looked down at the water. "I will, if I need to." She reached for her pack and secured it. "We'll run a rope between us. There won't be any light until we can get above surface again."

Mikell liked the plan less by the moment. Underwater for an unknown length of time without even being able to see where they were going? But as Ari said, they didn't have any other options. He took a deep breath. This was the only way to find Mara. He would do whatever it took. He wouldn't let an angry fight be the last words between them.

"You should lead," Korent said, handing Ari the end of a rope. "Of the three of us, you're the most likely to be able to tell which way we're going in the dark."

"To an extent." She took the rope and secured it around her waist. "Ready?"

Mikell finished tying himself to the other end of the rope. "Ready."

Korent, already secured to the rope between the others, took the torch. "We don't really know how many of these we'll need. Better keep it." He climbed into the water.

The frigid water hit Mikell like a jolt of lightning to his whole body as he followed, though the river only reached to his waist. An instinctive gasp tore loose from his lips. The other two shivered as much as he did, making the torchlight flicker in a disconcerting way.

"On three," Ari said, her voice made choppy by the shivering. "One... two... three."

Mikell sucked in a breath and dropped beneath the surface, the glow of the torch vanishing at the same time. He felt a tug at the rope and swam in that direction, the current helping him along. Good thing they weren't trying to fight their way upstream. He didn't think he would have made it.

His lungs ached. He couldn't tell how long they had been under the surface. It felt like hours, but he knew it couldn't be more than a minute. With each stroke, his hands brushed against the smoothed rock cradling the river. Then his hands hit rock on the upstroke. The space was narrowing.

The impulse to panic asserted itself, and he shoved it back down. He had to maintain presence of mind. The current wouldn't be flowing unless there was a way through.

He had to adapt his swimming as the space grew too narrow for his normal style, until he was essentially pulling himself along on uneven places of the rock floor. He couldn't tell where the others were. Desperation for air set in, clawing at the insides of his lungs, his throat, his mouth.

His arms hit more rock, and he had to feel around to find the low opening. The rope pulled hard at his waist as he struggled to squeeze through. His pack caught on something, and white encroached on the edges of the blackness, bringing a fresh sense of panic. He was stuck, and he was going to pass out. He kicked harder, pushing against any surface he could find. Something gave, releasing the hold on his pack, and he managed to slide free. It was a struggle just to move his arms now. He wasn't going to make it.

A faint blue glow ahead battled the whiteness. Light. That meant surface. Mikell clawed for it, kicking madly. The rope around his waist turned taut again, dragging him upward, and his head broke surface. He coughed and gasped in air, spitting water. Ari and Korent struggled beside him, their own breathing just as ragged as his.

They were in a broad cavern with some sort of glowing stones scattered across half the ceiling. It was hard to see far in the dim blue light, but it was enough to see they were in a deep pool with nothing but rock wall on three sides. On the fourth side, a slope rose out of the water and levelled out to form a floor for the other half of the cavern. The ceiling glow only covered the pool, and the other half was hard to see clearly, but it looked safe enough.

Mikell turned his body toward the slope and dragged at the water, but his limbs were sluggish. His muscles ached and threatened to give out and send him back beneath the surface.

"I can't—" Korent's voice came out weak and raspy as he struggled to swim.

The current had all but vanished in the deep pool, but now it picked up again, dragging them along. It was too strong for Mikell to maintain surface, and he barely managed to suck in a breath before slipping under.

It was only for a moment, though, as the water smacked him against the slope, then receded, leaving his head clear. He sucked in air as he pulled himself forward until only his lower half was still submerged. Good enough. He closed his eyes and focused on his breathing, trying to gather his strength.

Korent wheezed beside him. "Ari, you all right?"

She sounded even more exhausted than before. "I'm fine."

"Are you sure? Creating that wave didn't take too much energy?"

"I said I'm fine." Even through the exhaustion, she sounded vaguely amused. "Quit mothering."

Mikell felt a nudge at his good arm as Korent spoke again. "You dead, snitface?"

"Yeah."

"Oh, good."

Mikell groaned and pushed himself up, finally pulling himself the rest of the way out of the water. Ari sat on the level, her legs trailing down the slope as she arduously wrung out her mass of hair. The dim, bluish light made her paleness look even worse. Korent lay on the slope just beside her, working on untying the rope from his waist without putting much effort into it.

Mikell climbed the slope and plopped down on the level surface, pulling the rope free from his own waist and then checking his pack, which now had a long, jagged tear in it. He groaned again. "My pack tore down there. I'm not sure how much I have left."

"Torches?" Korent asked. "I get the feeling we aren't going to find much wood and oil to make our own down here."

"Food and water, too," Ari said. "The water in here is... less than clean."

Mikell made a face, flinging water off his good arm and wiping his face clear before setting to work inventorying his bag. No torches, but he still had most of his food and water, at least. He repacked his bag, but paused at the end, listening.

Korent eyed him. "Something wrong?"

Mikell pressed a finger over his lips, searching the space around them. It came again, a hissing noise he couldn't quite place, nor tell exactly where it came from.

The others heard it, too. "What is it?" Ari whispered.

Korent shook his head. "I don't know. Let's get some light over there and check it out." He stood, Mikell beside him, and ignited the oily rag on the end of his torch. The dunking in the river only momentarily delayed the flame.

The hissing thundered through the room as dark lumps of fur covering the ceiling and walls in the dark half of the cavern shifted away from the sudden light. Mikell grabbed the handle of his sword. It was hard to tell as the creatures clung to the walls and ceiling, but as best as he could see, they had small, round, furry bodies, long arms, and flat heads with dark eyes glaring from lowered eyelids. Underdwellers. They had to be.

A single opening led out of the cavern, and it was on the far wall. They'd have to walk underneath the creatures to get out. His grip on his sword tightened. How long had the underdwellers been there, watching them?

Ari slowly stood. "Mikell, Korent," she said quietly, "take your hands off your swords." She took a half step forward, raising empty hands. "We aren't here to hurt you." Her words were measured in a soft, comforting tone. "We are no threat to you. Let us pass."

"Do you think they understand you?" Korent whispered.

"I have no idea," she whispered back.

Mikell put his hands up in a similar gesture to Ari's, his gaze rapidly taking it all in from a tactician's perspective. The only possible retreat would be back into the water. They had barely survived the trip while the current was helping them; he doubted they would survive a return attempt. If the underdwellers decided to attack, they'd have no choice but to fight. Ari didn't look like she was in any shape to do anything, so that left him and Korent against a few dozen of these things. To their advantage, the creatures seemed primitive and might not have the skills to stand against trained fighters. Still, it would be best to avoid a fight if possible, seeing how greatly outnumbered they were.

The creatures still hadn't made any move in their direction. Mikell picked up his pack and slid it on as best as he could, hoping it wouldn't dump out even more of their supplies. Korent and Ari gathered their things as well, keeping their eyes on the underdwellers.

"What do you think?" Korent whispered.

"Only one way to find out," Ari replied. Keeping her hands out and open, she slowly started toward the tunnel. Mikell and Korent followed, watching for the first sign of trouble. The creatures shifted around, but the hissing was decreasing. The ones closest to the torch in Korent's hand hissed louder at the light as he walked by.

They passed the halfway point. It wasn't much further to the exit. Mikell's hand wanted to go for his sword, but he forced himself to stay focused. As long as they showed they were no threat, it seemed the creatures would let them pass. Perhaps this was a more peaceful tribe of underdwellers than the ones he'd heard the stories about. It wouldn't be much longer before he and his companions were out of the cavern and away from these things.

The mass of creatures moved so abruptly that Mikell had the disturbing sensation of the walls shifting around him. He froze as the underdwellers crawled down from the walls toward their sides and jumped from the ceiling to land behind them, none of them too close, but all glaring, crouching on their short legs and hissing.

Mikell shot a glance ahead. The creatures had filled in the space in front of the tunnel as well, surrounding them.

"Wait." Ari's tone was urgent but low. "They might be testing us to see if we're a threat. Keep your hands clear." Mikell looked around at the dark eyes reflecting torchlight back at him. Was it malice in their eyes, or defensiveness? He couldn't tell. He let his fingers curl just slightly, prepared to draw his sword the instant the creatures moved.

The hissing intensified, and the creatures shifted forward, narrowing the circle around them. "They aren't going to let us go," Mikell whispered, slowly moving his hand closer to his blade.

"We aren't here to hurt you," Ari said to the creatures once more. "Please let us through."

The hiss unified, and the underdwellers attacked. Mikell yanked his sword free, knocking one back in the process. Korent kicked at one while swinging at another.

A massive wave roared around the outer edge of the room, gaining speed as it followed the curve toward the tunnel, and swept away the creatures between them and their escape route. "Run!" Ari shouted, already moving at her fastest hobble. Korent and Mikell followed her in retreat, swinging at grasping arms from the underdwellers still standing. The hissing turned into snarls, and the creatures swarmed after them.

"Faster," Mikell barked, swinging behind himself to dissuade one of the creatures from getting as close as it had. Another set of fingers barely missed grabbing his foot. They were going too slowly. In her weakened state, Ari couldn't run as fast as they needed. Besides, they couldn't see more than a few paces ahead at a time as they raced through the labyrinthine tunnels. Any faster, and they might not see hazards in time to avoid them.

He glanced back once more. The creatures were charging, snarling, and gaining. There wasn't much choice.

Mikell grabbed Ari around the waist and sped up, all but dragging her along with him, though his shoulder screamed in protest. Korent kept pace right behind them, keeping the torch as high as he could while swinging his sword to the rear to keep the underdwellers from getting too close.

The light reflected off solid wall ahead, and Mikell banked hard to the right. Another right, then a left. Jagged rocks protruded from the ceiling and walls, forcing them to duck and dodge, but Mikell refused to slow down. Another right. He barely saw the raised ledge in time to jump up onto it rather than kneecapping himself. A lower tunnel dropped off to the right, and he took it, forcing Ari to move at a slight crouch. Then a left.

"Here," Korent hissed. "That corner ahead! Ari, the torch!"

Mikell saw it and took it, finding himself facing a narrow passage. Korent squeezed in behind Mikell and Ari. Ari lifted a hand, and the torchlight disappeared. If the underdwellers came around the corner, no doubt their dark vision would reveal the three of them standing there. But with any hope, without the torchlight reflecting off the nearby walls and corners, the underdwellers wouldn't figure out which corner they'd taken.

They held still, fighting to keep their breathing quiet and even, though Mikell's side ached so badly he wanted to drop to his knees and suck in air as fast as he could. His shoulder felt like it had been torn in two.

Hissing snarls echoed from a distance, but never came close. They'd lost the underdwellers. Mikell closed his eyes and leaned back against the cold rock wall, letting himself catch his breath at an easier rate.

They stayed there in the silent darkness for an uncomfortably long time before Korent broke it. "Think it's safe?"

"It's been long enough," Mikell agreed. "They would have found us by now if they were going to, I think."

The light flared back to life. "Now what?" Korent asked.

"We keep going." Mikell took off his pack to secure the torn piece better. It looked like he hadn't lost too much in their mad dash. "Mara's still out there, somewhere."

His hands paused, then tightened. Mara was lost in this cave system infested by hostile, murderous underdwellers. What would she do if they came after her? She would be all alone. They'd tear her apart. "We have to find her." He fixed his pack the best he could, anxious to get moving.

Ari slumped against the wall, and Korent caught her before she fell to the ground. "Ari?" He gripped her tighter. "Ari!"

She startled awake. "I'm okay."

"No, you're not, and you know it. You've used too much energy," Korent chided. He looked at Mikell. "She needs rest. We all do."

Mikell looked back at the dark tunnels. If only Mara was there, it wouldn't be a problem. "Mara. I can't just leave her on her own."

"She's likely to be on her own for a while, brother. I'm sorry to say it, but as big as these caverns are, the chance of finding her soon is miniscule. And we won't do her any good if we drive ourselves past the point of exhaustion."

Mikell scowled, but even he could tell Ari was about to pass out again. His shoulder joined the argument with a sharp throb. Korent was right. They'd be able to move faster and easier after they'd had some time to recover. He sighed. "Very well."

Korent clapped him on the good shoulder, then continued forward through the narrow passage, helping Ari along behind him. "Besides, Mara is a smart, strong woman. She'll figure out a way to avoid danger."

Mikell looked back. "I only hope you're right."

Chapter 8

Mara strained, feeling the rock wall above her for another handhold. The low tunnel she traveled through occasionally opened up into a narrow crevasse again before closing back down into a tunnel, giving her hope of climbing back up the sheer crevasse wall to the first ledge they'd walked on. Each time, she'd failed. She only prayed this time would be different.

She stretched further, feeling the pain in her other hand as her fingers shook from the effort of keeping herself on the wall and keeping the torch relatively upright at the same time. The ache grew more demanding as she searched in vain for the next grip.

Nothing. And the wall on the other side of the crevasse was too far away to reach. She leaned her forehead against the cold rock. She would have to climb back down and keep moving. Again.

She shifted her weight and carefully made her way back down, but her foot slipped while just a shoulder-height above the ground. Her cheek smacked into the rock, her knee into the ground, and her palm into grit, the torch spinning crazily away before coming to a rest against the wall. She dropped onto her back and groaned. She wasn't cut out for this.

After a brief pity party, she brushed herself off, found more grit coating her body and limbs, and gave up on getting it all off. She couldn't imagine her face looked much better.

She sighed, pushing her hair back with filthy hands before picking up the torch once more. Time to move on.

The path from here sloped more steeply downward as it closed back up into a tunnel again. Mara had hoped she could climb her way free from the crevasse opening before having to take the path even further from Mikell and their friends. But there were no other options. The sometimes-tunnel-sometimes-crevasse path had no branches, just this one route. The tunnels were sometimes small enough to force her to crawl, sometimes tall enough she could stretch her arms above her without reaching anything, but always moving onward and downward.

"A little variety would be nice," she told it. "Maybe a branch or two going a different direction. Like upward."

It ignored her.

She sighed and continued on the steep path downward, going slowly and holding the torch out so she could watch her footing as she leaned back into the path. The ceiling closed once more, sinking low enough that she was almost lying flat as she scooted her way down. Fatigue encroached as the hours dragged by and the slope grew steeper, forcing her to go slower and keep tight control over her downward slide.

The rocks shifted under her foot without warning. She flung out a hand to find a grip, but she was already sliding out of control, smacking against one side or the other as she dropped. The ground leveled out, and she tumbled over herself several times before finally coming to a stop.

She lay stunned for a minute, then cautiously attempted movement. The pain in her arm made her groan. She allowed just a touch of healing energy to tend to it, then tried again, managing to get herself into an upright seated position this time. She was going to have some bruises, no question. The torch lay a few paces from her, the light flickering dimly as if to protest the rough landing. She sighed and crawled over to pick it up.

A hairy hand clamped around her arm as she lifted the torch. Pointed teeth glistened in the light as a creature yanked her forward with a snarl, snapping at her. She screamed and dropped backwards, kicking over and over as hard as she could. The grip on her arm loosened, and she scrambled back until she ran into the rock wall.

Her attacker didn't pursue her. She sucked in air, trying to steady her pounding heart. The torchlight didn't reach far enough to see where the thing had gone, what it was doing, or why it hadn't chased her. Maybe it had only been startled by her getting near, and now that she was away from it, it wasn't threatened anymore. She doubted that was the case.

It took another moment before she gathered enough courage to raise the torch higher and lean forward, trying to see. The hairy arm swiped at her again, making her jump, but it was too far away to be any real threat.

She cautiously stood and took another step forward. The light finally reached far enough for her to see a round, hairy body topped by a flat head, the creature cringing away from the light and hissing. Mara's breath caught. It must be an underdweller. The overly long arm that had swiped at her shielded its eyes, and the other arm seemed stretched back behind a rock. Mara took another cautious step. The creature snarled and swung at her, straining to reach, but the other arm kept it from moving any closer.

"You're trapped," Mara whispered in realization. She moved around, keeping a careful distance, and saw she was right. The underdweller's other arm was pinned between two rocks. The creature kept straining to grab her, but there was no way for it to move any closer. She was safe.

She took a moment to check her surroundings. It wasn't a very big room, but large enough that she could get around without coming in reach of the creature, though she would have to duck in a couple places to avoid rocky protrusions. Only one other tunnel led out, opposite the tunnel she'd tumbled through, and still going downward. Disappointing, but at least this one had a gentler slope.

She started toward the tunnel, but stopped, looking back at the underdweller. She couldn't just leave it trapped like that. It would be foolish to go near it again, much less to help it. It was an underdweller, and clearly as vicious as the stories had indicated. Mikell would say it would just attack her again, so it was too dangerous to try.

But even if that was true, she still couldn't bring herself to walk away.

She dug one of the spare torches out of her damaged pack and carefully circled around, testing the distance until she found an angle where she could get close enough to the rock without the underdweller being able to reach her. It kicked and scrambled at the rock, trying to lash out at her, but the angle made it impossible.

I should leave it alone. It will attack me if I try to free it. She looked at it, the rock, and the tunnel. Maybe the creature would be grateful for being freed and wouldn't hurt her. Maybe it would be too injured to make much of a pursuit. Maybe she could shift the rock enough for the creature to get free, then dash to the tunnel before it recovered enough to come after her.

Mara took a deep breath, wedged the torch into the crack between the rocks, and pushed down on the end with all her might. Nothing happened. She leaned on it, trying to drive her full body weight into the tiny lever.

For a moment, it still didn't move, but then it budged a fraction. And another. Encouraged, she pushed harder, keeping an eye on the underdweller. As soon as it was free, she would have to move fast. But the creature seemed to have realized what she was doing; it was leaning into the rock and straining to push it along with her. Another budge, then another, and the creature squirmed its arm free.

Mara released the rock and bolted for the tunnel, ducking low to avoid banging her head. A hand caught her leg, tripping her flat. Her torch rolled across the floor and stopped a pace away. The underdweller tore its way along her, claws digging into her flesh, and she screamed, pushing herself over to kick and flail at it. It wrapped the long fingers of its good hand around her neck and squeezed, cutting off her air.

She struggled and fought to pull its hand away, but it was too strong. She tried to dig her fingers under its thumb to pull from there. The creature snapped at her, clamping sharp teeth around her wrist.

It was getting hard to think straight, to do anything. There had to be a way to break free. There was only one thing she could do, and with any hope, the adrenaline and panic would be enough to make it work. She grabbed the creature's arm with her other hand and focused on Tashan's words. Connection to block adrenaline. Healing to bring calm. A nudge to bring sleep.

The creature stumbled backwards, releasing her. She coughed and sucked in air, stinging her injured throat. It had worked!

No time to celebrate; she had to get away before the creature recovered. She struggled upward, but the creature was already there, blocking the exit and snarling threateningly.

Her heart sank. It hadn't worked. It had only dazed the thing for a moment. Better than she'd managed last time, but still not enough. The underdweller took another step forward as if to test her.

Her mind raced. She couldn't fight it. She couldn't put it to sleep. It was going to kill her unless she came up with something else, fast. It bared those sharp teeth at her again, taking another step closer. Mara's hand instinctively went to her injured wrist. Her gaze flicked to the creature's own mangled arm. It was bent at unnatural angles from where the rock had crushed it, and it dragged limply on the ground. The thing was hurt. Scared. The thought was crazy, but maybe it was lashing out because of the pain. Maybe if she healed it...

Definitely crazy. It would just become stronger and able to kill her easier. She glanced back at the low tunnel behind her. There was no way she could climb faster than an underdweller. She couldn't escape. Couldn't fight. Healing was the only other option, crazy though it might be.

She reached out a hand, and the creature flinched back a half-step. When she had first tried healing at a distance, it had taken more energy than she could manage. But she'd practiced, and while it took extra focus, it no longer depleted her as it once had.

The creature took another stumbling step backward, looking at its shattered limb in alarm. It clawed at it with the other hand as if trying to tear away the strange warmth it felt. It snarled as the flesh repaired itself, then fell over backwards and tried to scoot away as the bones slid back into place.

Mara finished and hesitated, unsure how the creature would react. It stared at its arm, slowly moving the muscles and testing its fingers. If she was going to get away, now was her chance while it was distracted. She cautiously moved in a slow circle, keeping her eyes on the creature. It ignored her as she passed it. She walked sideways, then backwards, only occasionally glancing over her shoulder to make sure she wasn't about to walk into a rock.

She retrieved her torch and reached the tunnel, stepped in, and moved slowly a few more paces as the creature disappeared from her view. It took a moment to gather the courage to turn around, then she bolted. She couldn't go too fast with the downward slope—she didn't want to take another tumble—but she took it as fast as she dared. The more distance she could put between herself and the creature, the better. She kept her torch high, watching for any dangers and occasionally glancing backwards, sure she would see the creature loping after her, claws and fangs ready for the attack.

She wasn't sure how long she ran until she finally slowed, panting. It was okay. The underdweller wasn't chasing her. She was safe. She kept walking at an easier pace and caught her breath. She'd have to watch closely in case there were more of those things here. There probably were—they were probably everywhere in the cavern system. What if they went after Mikell and the others?

She pushed back the worry, reminding herself that the other three were strong fighters. She was the only one who couldn't really defend herself. She sighed.

A faint sound seemed to carry beneath her sigh. Mara froze and looked back, straining her ears and eyes, trying to detect where the sound had come from. Nothing.

She frowned and resumed walking. The mystery sound promptly returned. She spun, determined to catch it this time, but the tunnel behind her was still empty. She turned in place, torch extended, checking the walls, the shadows of jutting rocks behind her. Something was there, she knew it. She just couldn't find it.

She took one more look around, then glanced up. The underdweller looked back at her from where it clung to the ceiling. She screamed and bolted, but her foot caught on an uneven spot, flattening her.

The creature dropped beside her with a thump. She screamed again, scrambling backwards, the torch flashing crazily as she moved. It hadn't worked. The creature had come after her, and now it was going to kill her. Its arm lashed forward, and she cringed away. But the strike never landed. She hesitated, unsure, then took a cautious peek.

The creature stood in front of her, holding out the unlit torch she'd used as a lever to free it. No snarls or hisses this time, and no bared teeth. She stared, uncertain how to react. It pushed its hands a little closer, so she carefully reached out and took the torch.

The underdweller shrugged, then reached out again with both hands. It held what looked like some sort of green, mossy growth. Mara stared once more. It waved the green thing at her, pushing its hands even closer this time.

"Okay, okay," she said quickly, and she took the moss.

Another shrug. The creature stared at her, seeming to be waiting for something.

"Um... Thank you?" She turned the chunk of moss over in her hands. The top was dry, but the bottom felt unpleasantly moist. She did her best not to show revulsion. "It's very nice."

An awkward silence dragged on. The creature looked at her, then the moss, then her again, still waiting. Finally, it raised a hand to its mouth as if eating something.

Mara's stomach lurched. "You want me to eat it?" The underdweller kept its intense stare on her. She managed to keep her groan internal. She'd gotten on the thing's good side, it seemed. She couldn't ruin it now. She lifted the moss toward her mouth, but stopped at one sniff. The tangy but almost putrid smell was overwhelming, triggering a gag reflex. She lowered her hand, taking deep breaths and trying not to vomit.

The creature snarled, but without the teeth baring and threatening posture of before. It took her a moment to realize that the snarling sound rose and fell, taking on different tones. It was talking to her. It thrust its face closer, then repeated the eating pantomime, with firmer motions this time.

No way around it. If she wanted to keep the underdweller happy, she had to take a bite. It took her a moment to gather her resolve, then she lifted the moss and took the smallest bite possible, cringing as she did so.

She blinked in surprise. It was delicious. The texture was like a crisp form of lactuca, and the flavor was sweet and tangy. She hadn't realized until that moment how hungry she was, and she consumed the whole chunk in just a few bites. The creature shrugged again and danced around in a funny circle, waving its arms over its head.

"Oh," she said as realization struck. "You're happy, aren't you?" The shrug must be how underdwellers showed that they were pleased. She sat up straighter, finding a fresh sense of alertness after eating the moss. "Do you understand me? My name is Mara."

The dance stopped, and the creature stared at her.

She pointed to herself. "Mara." Again, "Ma-ra."

It looked her over, then spoke in the snarling voice. "Nahnah."

"Close," she said, encouraged. "Ma-ra."

"Nahnah."

"Mah-rah."

"Nah-nah."

She thought a moment, then nodded. "Okay. Nahnah. What about you? What's your name?"

It stared again.

"I'm Mara," she pointed at herself, then at it. "What's your name?"

The underdweller pointed at her. "Nahnah." Its eyes seemed to widen as if with understanding, and it poked its chest. "Lut."

She hesitated, unsure she'd heard the consonants correctly through the snarling sound. "Lut?"

It shrugged and resumed the dance.

Mara smiled, feeling encouraged. It—perhaps he?—was no longer trying to kill her, and they had managed some basic communication. "You live down here, I'm guessing. So you must know your way around these tunnels." She looked around, then pointed upward and back toward where she believed Mikell and the others would be. "I'm trying to go there to find my friends. Can you help me?"

He stopped dancing and stared once more.

"Hmm." She thought, then spoke slower. "My friends," she mimed a hug, careful not to get the torch too close to her body, "are missing, and I need to find them," she mimed looking around with a hand pressed against her forehead. "Can you help me?" she finished, pointing first at him, then herself.

Lut stared a moment longer, then jumped at her. She flinched away from the attack, but instead found him clinging to her arm as if hugging it, both of his arms wrapped tight around hers and his head nestled close. "O-kay. Maybe not." She set the torch down and gently pried his arms away. "Thank you. That was very sweet." Not helpful, though. Oh, well. She was just grateful he wasn't trying to kill her anymore. "Thank you for the food and bringing me my torch. I need to go find my friends now." She stood, brushed herself off, and started down the tunnel again.

Lut followed her.

She looked down at him, his head bobbing at just above her waist level. "I guess you're all alone, too. Were you separated from your friends?" She neither expected nor received an answer. "Okay. Maybe we'll find our friends together."

Something in the back of her mind told her she was foolish and should get away from Lut as soon as she possibly could. Finding more like him most likely meant getting attacked again, seeing how that was his instinctive response to her. She would part ways with him, she decided. But no reason to rush it. Lut was sweet, in an odd way, and there was nothing wrong with making her way through the cave system with him at her side.

They didn't make it far before her steps began dragging. She hadn't realized how exhausted she was, likely because of all the adrenaline she'd been subject to in the last while. It was impossible to tell for sure in the dark cave, of course, but she had a feeling it was well after dark outside.

The tunnel showed no signs of branching or opening up into a proper room, but she saw a small alcove of sorts just ahead. She angled for it, then sat down. "I need to rest," she said, then leaned her head against her hands as if sleeping and made a faint snoring sound.

Lut stared for a moment, then made a choppy hissing sound, shrugging repeatedly. It took her a moment to realize he was laughing. Perhaps the hand gesture meant something else to his kind, or was simply foreign and strange to him. It was hard to say for sure. She was trying to come up with another way to communicate the need when Lut scooted past her, patted around the alcove wall, then nestled in against the rocks at one end of the space, curling his arms around himself like a treeape in its nest.

"You do understand," Mara said, relieved. She pressed to the back of the alcove as far as she could and settled down against the wall. There was still a thin blanket in the bottom of her pack, to her relief. It was made from veelish wool, soft and incredibly warm for being so thin.

Grateful, she wrapped it around herself and rested her head on her pack as a pillow. Mikell would be horrified if he knew she was sleeping just a pace away from a creature who had tried to kill her not long before. But her instincts told her Lut wasn't going to hurt her now. Healing him had earned his trust, and she trusted him in return. She closed her eyes and let sleep take her.

Chapter 9

M*ikell*

A sudden bright light and sensation of warmth yanked Mikell from his sleep. Ari sat to his left, focusing on a rotating sphere of fire in the middle of the small cave room they'd found to rest in. "What are you doing? They might see that!" he hissed, though he knew some of his outrage was due to his own foolishness at falling asleep when he was supposed to be keeping watch.

"We'll all die of the cold if we don't warm up," Ari replied without taking her eyes off the sphere.

He realized he'd still been dripping wet when they stopped to rest, but now was completely dry. The rock surface leading out of their hiding space glistened damply. "Did you use your magic on me?"

"Hush. This takes concentration. Unless you want me to lose control of the fire."

Mikell scowled, but reluctantly let himself soak in the warmth. She was right; they needed to warm themselves. He hadn't realized how little he could feel in his hands and feet until they started tingling as they thawed.

Korent yawned and stretched from the other side of the space, sitting up and blinking the last of the sleep from his eyes. "Doesn't fire take a lot out of you? And after you drained yourself before—"

"Quit mothering. I'm using it sparingly."

Korent seemed to consider that, then shrugged and leaned back, basking in the heat. "Okay." He dug out some food and put a portion in front of Ari before chomping into his own.

Mikell eyed the large ball of fire as he found some food for himself. If that was 'sparing,' he didn't want to know what 'normal' looked like. "I got turned around while we were running. Any idea which way we should go?"

"None at all," Korent said in that annoyingly cheerful way.

"I barely remember any of that." Ari shifted one hand, and the sphere shrank to the size of a fist.

Mikell shivered at the sudden change in temperature. "Can't we warm up more?"

"The caves are going to be cold no matter what," Ari said, transferring the fire onto a torch end, letting the oil take over from there. "I can't maintain a personal fire to follow us around and keep us warm. I believe we've all warmed back to normal, yes? If we get any warmer, the caves will feel even colder by contrast." She smiled at Korent as she picked up the food he'd gotten out for her.

Mikell flexed his fingers. She was right. He felt cold, but he was no longer near-frozen as he'd been before. He pulled his dry cloak tighter around himself. "Is Mara still okay? I don't know how long we were asleep. Can you tell if she's all right?"

"She's still alive."

Korent met his eyes. "We'll find her. I promise."

Mikell nodded, determined to make that promise a reality no matter what it took. "Let's go."

They took their time, checking around corners before proceeding and always keeping an eye on the ceiling for any signs of furry lumps. Mikell would have liked to move faster, but the caution was necessary. If they got killed by underdwellers, they'd never find Mara.

Besides, Ari was still limping. His left shoulder ached all the more, and a few new bruises had asserted themselves. Korent didn't look that much better. They wouldn't have been able to go much faster even if they wanted to.

The tunnel ahead ended on a new tunnel running perpendicular to theirs. Mikell checked around the corner, looking right and left, and found it empty. "Which way?"

"Does it matter? It's going to be a guess either way," Korent pointed out.

"He's right," Ari said. "I don't see anything to indicate one way as better than the other."

Mikell eyed the two directions again. "This way seems to go down," he said, gesturing to the left. His shoulder yelled at him for the abrupt movement, and he winced. It had been a long time since any pain or injury lingered. Mara was always there to chase it away with her warm touch. He felt a fresh pang that had nothing to do with his physical injuries. She was alone, somewhere, in a cave infested by homicidal creatures. And the last time they spoke... His harsh, angry words kept rattling back through his mind, condemning him with each syllable.

"Do we want to go down? Or should we be trying to make our way up, back to the ledge we started on?" Korent asked.

Ari seemed to consider both directions. She closed her eyes, concentrating. After several motionless seconds, she opened her eyes, blinking and drawing in a deep breath as if waking from a deep sleep. "Down. She's down."

"You found her?" Hope welled up in Mikell's heart.

"I can't do the trick well enough to actually see her, but I know she's that way," Ari pointed to the upward slope on the right, "and down." She pointed to the downward slope on the left.

Mikell blew out an irritated breath. How were they going to find Mara in this massive cave system? It seemed all the more impossible by the moment. "So we should go right and find a way down from there."

"No," Ari said, turning to the left. "I sensed movement in that direction, and lots of it. Most likely more of the underdwellers. We'll go down first, then try to work our way back across."

The tunnel to the left sloped more steeply downward the further they went, then leveled out in a small room. A faint trickling sound revealed a tiny stream of water running down the wall, disappearing into an opening at the bottom. Ari cupped some in her hands. "It's clean. Drink up and fill your waterskins."

Part of Mikell didn't want to stop, but the rest of him already wanted a break. His shoulder ached as he collected the water, and he sat down on a rise in the floor as soon as he was done.

Korent plopped down beside him. "Still in one piece?"

"Somehow." Mikell rubbed at a sore spot on his side. "Do you think Mara's doing okay? She wouldn't know how to tell if a water source is clean or not. She might not even be near a water source." More thoughts flashed through his mind, dropping new worries like weights on his chest. "What if she—"

Korent gripped Mikell's good shoulder. "By Maker's favor, she's still alive, remember? And Mara is a smart woman. She'll find a way to take care of herself. You have to trust that."

"I know. I just—" Mikell sighed, words failing him.

"You worry about the ones you love," Ari said, compassion in her voice. "It's only natural." She finished collecting water. "We'll find her. I'm certain."

"How?" For the first time in his life, he actually wanted magic to be the answer, for Ari to say that she had some way of instantly locating his wife.

"Because." Her tone had a refreshed sense of mission and determination. "We're going to find the green stone. It amplifies magic abilities. Once we have it, I can use it to find her."

Mikell stood. "Then let's find it." He paused. "How?"

"Same as before. We'll still try to make our way toward Mara, and I'll keep my energy open to watch for more places of imbued magic."

"Sounds like a plan." Korent took one more drink from the stream. The others did the same before they moved on out of the room. The tunnel dropped lower again, narrowing to the point they had to take off their packs and turn sideways to get through. Mikell kept watching for a branch they could take, but nothing appeared. He was relieved when the space finally widened again. The tight space had been getting claustrophobic.

As if to prove itself a study in opposites, the tunnel abruptly opened outward on one side, with nothing but blackness in that direction. They stopped and checked over the ledge their path now formed.

"This feels familiar," Korent said. He found a bit of loose rock and tossed it over the side. It made no sound.

Ari moved closer to the edge and looked upward, craning her neck to see around the overhang. "I think this is the same cavern we were walking along before."

"Probably," Korent agreed. "It'd be awfully coincidental to have two massive, unending caverns inside the same mountain."

"Maybe we should go back," Mikell said, eying the ledge ahead with suspicion. He wasn't sure they could trust it to hold their weight after what happened with the previous one.

"Really?" Korent asked, giving him a look. "Back through all of that, and toward more underdwellers?"

"At least we'd be going the right way toward Mara, and not trusting our lives to an unstable ledge."

"The tunnel bent a few times along the way," Ari pointed out. "We may be closer to the right direction than you think."

"Then check," Mikell said.

Ari looked regretful. "We don't know what we're going to encounter ahead. I can't risk using that much energy."

Mikell scowled. "Then what good are you?"

"Hey," Korent snapped.

Ari put a hand up before either of them could say more. "We're all hurt and frustrated, and you're worried about your wife. We all are. The best thing we can do is stay together and focus on moving forward."

Some of Mikell's ire swept away with her words. He nodded. "Right." A sense of familiarity thrummed through his mind. It was almost like how Mara always had the right words to say to calm him down. Perhaps his wife wasn't the only one changed by the connection.

Korent crouched and held his torch low over the edge, leaning slightly to examine the path ahead. "It looks like a more solid foundation than the last one. I think we'll be okay."

"And we'll be more careful this time," Ari added.

Mikell kept a close eye on the ground as they continued onward, slowing at every tiny crack he spotted. But Korent was right, and the ledge proved solid enough.

They'd been walking for some time when Mikell spotted a wider space ahead. The ledge seemed to turn upward at that point, but there was also something in the shadows on the cavern side of the path. As they got closer, their torchlight revealed it to be another ledge, joining this one here but then dropping downward even more steeply as it continued along the edge of the cavern.

"I still think down is the best way to go," Ari said, looking from one option to the other.

"I see no reason to think otherwise," Korent shrugged.

Mikell felt the same. "It's steep. We'll have to take it slowly."

"Just stay close to the wall, and we should be fine," Korent said.

Mikell kept a hand on the wall, curling his fingers around handholds as they carefully descended. If he slipped, he wouldn't let himself tumble into the others and knock all three of them down—or possibly over the edge. His foot slid on the next step, but only for a fraction before finding a solid position. He exhaled and drew in a slow breath to steady his now-rapid heartbeat, then took another step.

A hissing sound echoed through the cavern. Mikell froze and looked up, then down, trying to spot the source. The other two leaned into the wall, looking around and listening in the silence. Mikell strained his ears, and after a moment, the hiss came again.

"They're above us," he whispered as quietly as he could.

Ari nodded, resuming the trek down the path a little faster now. "We have to get out of the open. They could climb straight down to us and throw us over the side."

She was right—it was either risk slipping by moving faster or risk being caught in such a vulnerable position by the underdwellers. Mikell picked up the pace, still doing his best to grip any protrusions he could find as he went. Still, the others got distance ahead of him. The path's slope decreased to a mild angle downward, to Mikell's relief.

The torch in his hand suddenly went out, the other torches extinguishing at the same moment. He froze, the relief vanishing as he clung to the wall. "What happened?"

"Quiet." Ari's voice was barely audible. "Keep moving along the wall and stay silent."

Mikell shuffled his feet forward, one after the other, gripping the wall all the more tightly. The torches did make them more visible, but he wasn't convinced it would make enough of a difference with them extinguished. It seemed this would be more of a hindrance to them than to the dark-seeing creatures. His hand reached for the wall ahead and hit air, an edge catching him across the forearm. He groped blindly. Had the path taken a sharp turn?

"Get in," Korent hissed, keeping his voice as quiet as possible. Mikell felt a hand wrap around his wrist and tug him forward. He stretched his other hand out and found the edges of the wall. It seemed like they'd found a crevice to hide in.

"Shouldn't we keep going?" he whispered.

A hissing sound interrupted before the others could voice their opinions. It was closer now, too close. Mikell clamped his mouth shut and pressed himself against the wall, keeping his breathing steady and his hand on his sword. With any hope, the creatures hadn't seen them. With any hope, the threat would pass and they could resume their search for Mara and the stone. With any hope, Mara hadn't run into any of the underdwellers.

His mind reverberated on one thought: *Maker watch her.*

Chapter 10

Mara kept her torch high as she resumed the walk down the tunnel, feeling significantly better after resting. Lut ambled beside her, occasionally jabbering in his snarling way. Even though she couldn't understand a word he said, it was comforting to have someone to talk to.

She spotted another tunnel branching off to the left ahead. "Where do you think that leads?"

Lut jabbered.

"Yeah, let's check it out." Mara stopped at the intersection and waved her torch even higher, trying to see as far as she could. The new route was wider than this one, and to her delight, it sloped upwards ahead. "Perfect." She beckoned Lut to follow her. "This way."

Lut sniffed loudly at the tunnel and snarled.

"What? You don't want to go that way?"

Another snarl.

"Well, this is the way I need to go. It's okay if you don't want to come with me." Mara felt a small pang at the thought of losing her new traveling companion, but she'd already known they would have to part ways sooner or later. She took a moment to seek out Mikell again, once more seeing nothing in the darkness. Worry took residence in her chest. Shouldn't he have lit a torch by now? Had he been unconscious this whole time? How badly hurt was he?

She took a deep breath, trying to push the anxious thoughts away. He could just be resting, like she had. He could be fine. All she knew for sure was that he was still somewhere above her. Up was the only choice. "I have to go this way," she repeated as she started along the new path.

Lut sniffed again, his snarl taking an almost grumbling tone, then he caught up and resumed walking beside her. She felt a stronger relief than she'd expected. "Thank you."

The tunnel sloped gently at first, then steeper, then so steep she had to use her hands as much as her feet, working from bump to bump. Lut switched to crawling along the wall beside her.

She paused to catch her breath. How long had they been climbing? She could no longer see the gentler slope below, though that wasn't saying much in these pitch black caves. She leaned back and stretched the torch higher in hopes of seeing their path level out ahead. No luck, but she did see another route branching off to the left. She scaled up and was thrilled to see a far gentler slope, still moving upward. Perfect.

Lut sniffed again as Mara climbed into the easier tunnel. He made a hissing noise.

"What? What's wrong?"

He snarled, craning his neck.

Mara raised the torch higher and squinted, but saw nothing down the tunnel, just more rocks. It was perhaps damper than the previous tunnel, with the wet rocks reflecting light back at her, but there was nothing threatening about that.

Then she remembered that Lut had hissed at her before. Maybe he smelled Mikell and the others? Renewed hope washed through her. "It's okay if you don't want to come this way," she told him, then started forward.

She hadn't made it three steps before her foot stuck. She caught the wall for balance, and her hand landed on some cold gel that squished beneath her fingers. "Ugh!" She tried to yank her hand away, but it was stuck, too. The rocks weren't damp; they were covered in this weird gel.

Lut scrambled to her side, pulling at her free leg back toward the steeper tunnel. "I'm stuck," she strained out as she fought to push away from the stuff that held her hand and foot captive. He pulled harder, nearly toppling her over. "Hold on, let me get myself positioned better!" But of course he couldn't understand her, his jumping and yanking growing more frantic.

She managed to break free of his grip and plant her foot squarely, then put her other hand against a clear spot on the wall and pushed as hard as she could. Her stuck hand budged with a burning pain, like the gel was keeping a layer of skin with it. She clenched her teeth and pulled harder, unable to stop the cry of pain as she finally got her hand free.

She hugged her throbbing hand against her chest, taking deep breaths. Her energy instinctively probed at the hand, but there was no injury to heal. It still felt on fire, but it wasn't actually damaged.

Lut continued tugging at her, snarling and hissing. She took her torch with the newly freed hand and pushed against the wall once more, this time for leverage to free her foot. Lut gripped her ankle with both hands and pulled along with her. Her heel wobbled and peeled out of the gel.

A clicking sound echoed through the silent tunnels around them.

Lut shrieked and hissed, sending a barb of panic through Mara as he yanked even harder. She lost her balance and toppled onto her seat. The torch rolled free, teetered at the edge of the steep slope, and fell, plunging the tunnel into darkness. The clicking sound grew louder, competing with the sound of her own frantic breathing. She blindly grabbed at any rock protrusion she could reach, straining to break free.

Lut shrieked again, but the cry fell abruptly silent, and she felt him land on the floor beside her. A sharp pain jabbed into her neck, and the last thing she was aware of was her head hitting the solid rock floor.

Chapter 11

M*ikell* "Think they're gone?" Korent whispered. The last hissing sound had faded some time ago, though it was hard to say for sure how long they'd been waiting, huddled together in the dark.

Mikell strained his ears, tilting his head to listen. Silence. "I think—" A new sound came, distant and faint. He dropped his voice. "Still there." Korent's annoyed grunt was barely audible.

Mikell shared the sentiment. He itched to be back on the path, climbing downwards to find Mara. Who knows what she was up against while they stood around, doing nothing? His ear twitched, and he shifted his attention back to the sound. He frowned. That wasn't hissing. It sounded more like... "Footsteps," he whispered to the others. Though he couldn't see them, he sensed them tense and strain to hear.

The sound grew closer, and a voice carried after it. The distance made it hard to catch more than a few words at a time. "Incompetence! Absolute incompetence... lost them, and now we... stone by ourselves!"

Mikell gripped his sword. Someone else was trying to find the stone. He turned, ready to shout a challenge to the distant people above. Before he could step into the path, though, Ari caught his arm and Korent slapped a hand over his nose before readjusting down to cover his mouth. He sputtered and shoved at them as the sounds faded. Too late. He gave up the fight, and they released him.

After a long silence, Ari lit a torch. Mikell scowled at her, then Korent. "What was that for? Didn't you hear what they said? If they're looking for the stone, we need to know who they are and how they know of it. Are they enemies trying to find the stone before we do? Or allies who could help? We need to know."

"They aren't allies." Ari's voice was thin, her face pale. "I know that voice. It was Mundin."

Mikell stared at her. "That's not possible." Mundin? The one who betrayed the princess? "He was banished to Ebrun. The Hranites would have torn him apart for crossing them."

"He must have found a way to make a new deal with them," Ari said, her tone hardening. "Which tells us a lot about who he must have been speaking to."

Mikell's hand tightened on his sword. "Hranites? Here?" And Mara somewhere in these caves, alone and undefended. "Then why did you stop me?" he demanded. "We could have—"

"What? Slaughtered them all on the spot?" Korent shook his head. "We don't know how many there are. Better to know what we're up against before we just charge out swinging. What if he brought a hundred Hranites with him?"

"What would happen to Mara if we get ourselves killed rushing into a fight we can't win?" Ari asked.

Mikell clenched his teeth, but they were right. He scowled and released his sword. "And what if they find Mara before we do?"

"We'll find her first. Or we'll find the stone and deal with them when we know we can beat them," Ari said.

"And we don't even know if we're going the right way," Mikell muttered, stepping back onto the downward slope beside them. If the Hranites found Mara first, they'd kill her. And if they found the stone first, they would kill everyone.

Chapter 12

Something nudged Mara's leg. Squirmed, then nudged even harder. Her groan and shiver combined to create an odd mumbling sound. Why was she so cold? She reached to shove the heaviness of sleep away from her eyes—rather, she tried, but her hand wouldn't move. Nor would the other one. An alarm sounded in her head, and she forced her eyes open.

A faint blue glow reflected off shimmering gel coating the walls of the small alcove she lay in. The light came from rocks dotting those same walls and the ceiling above, most of them all but dripping with the gel, leaving only occasional spots untouched.

Disgust turned her stomach, and she tried to push herself upright. Her torso was stuck. She couldn't even lift her head, and she felt the cold sliminess against the back of her scalp. The only thing she could move were her legs. Panic coursed through her, and she opened her mouth to scream for help.

"Nahnah! Nahnah!" Lut's voice was urgent, insistent. He made a hissing noise that almost seemed cautionary rather than its usual threatening tone.

Mara forced herself to take deep breaths. Calm down, figure out the situation. She managed to tilt her head a fraction, just enough that she could strain her eyes to the very corners and see Lut trapped in the gel beside her, his feet turned toward her and his head further away. He had one arm free and was frantically pushing against the dry peak of a rock beside him, trying to peel the rest of his body clear.

She wiggled as much as she could. Kicking her legs wasn't getting her anywhere, but she did have one elbow, the one closest to Lut, that she could shift. The rest of her was stuck fast.

Lut managed to tear his foot, the one he'd been nudging her with, clear of the goo. He let out a long hissing sound in pain, then pushed again with his hand on the rock. Nothing. He panted, snuffling.

Mara tried, but she had no leverage to speak of. All she could do was hope Lut could get free and help her. But he already looked exhausted. It could have been the filtered blue light, but his face almost seemed paler than before.

She felt weaker than usual, herself. Likely a lingering effect from whatever substance had knocked them out. She focused on Lut, gathering her energies to send across the space and refresh him. With any hope, he'd be able to get them both free once he was back to full strength.

But her energy failed her. Even it was nearly depleted, to the degree she couldn't send it across to him. She'd have to touch him if she wanted to make any difference. She grunted in frustration.

A clicking noise echoed from the adjacent tunnel, and she froze. Lut stared, his eyes wide with fear. The clicking faded, and he resumed his frantic work.

Mara focused in a more physical way this time, driving all her strength into the arm closest Lut. She pushed her elbow against the clear spot with all her might, trying to budge her hand upward. The same tearing sensation as before shot through her skin, and she had to clench her teeth to keep from crying out. One finger pulled free. Then another.

The clicking sound returned, but she didn't stop, ignoring it and channeling everything she had into getting her hand free enough to reach Lut's foot only a fingerlength away. The side of her hand pulled free, and her forearm shifted. Lut pushed harder against the rock, and his foot budged closer. She threw her strength into one final thrust, and her fingertips landed on his hairy toes. It was the best chance she had. She released her healing energy.

Lut let out a tiny squawk in surprise. The clicking sound drew closer. He scrambled against the clean rock, his leg breaking clear first and helping push the rest of himself free. Mara looked back and forth between him and the tunnel, her heart pounding against her ribs. Whatever made the clicking noise had to be huge. Lut twisted, squirmed, and rolled free, placing his feet carefully to find the few places where the gel hadn't reached.

"Lut!" Mara whispered in relief. "Help me get free, quick!"

The clicking sound was joined by the rushing sound of movement, something brushing against rock as it neared. Lut gave another tiny squawk and bounced away, dancing from clean spot to clean spot.

"No! Lut, please," she begged, but he vanished behind a large mass of rock protruding from the floor.

The tunnel beside them filled with glistening, sleek blue shell. It shifted and turned as more and more lengths of segmented shell came into the space, dozens of legs coming from the snake-like body in pairs and even climbing the side of the tunnel to fit it all in. The first shell piece tilted upward, and she saw dozens of purplish eyes fixed on her. Beneath the rows of eyes, jagged mandibles snapped, and more gel dripped to the floor.

Mara couldn't have moved if she wanted to. Her body shook with terror. "Lut! LUT!" But he wasn't coming to help. She was on her own. Mara forced the panic back down. Panic would get her killed. She had to come up with a way out of this herself.

The monster's head bobbed closer, and she heard other clicking sounds further away down the tunnel. A distraction. If she could get the thing to turn its attention back that way, it would buy time for Lut to get her free so they could both escape. The redirection trick hadn't worked so well last time she tried it, but it was her only chance now.

She gathered the last dredges of her energy. Tashan had said it could work on animals and creatures, and while it was more likely to affect the less self-aware minds, it wasn't as precise, the results more likely to be something different than intended. She might convince it to check out the other sounds, or she might convince it to eat her faster.

She centered her focus on the creature's eyes and loosed the energy, easier to do than healing but still taking so much out of her that she feared she would faint before making any impact. Gritting her teeth, she concentrated, trying to think of what sort of impulses might coax an insectoid monster. *Need to see what that sound was. They might be coming for my prey. The prey is stuck. Find the sound, come back for the prey.* She repeated the thoughts over and over as darkness rimmed her vision.

The monster leaned closer, but stopped. It made a sharp clicking sound with its mandibles, snapping them together repeatedly. *It's going to eat me*, she thought numbly. *I'm going to die.* A blob of goo landed on her side, sinking the chill deep through her skin, and the air filled with clicking as the monster's multitudinous legs skittered over the walls, carrying it back down the tunnel away from them.

Relief brought with it a second wind. "Lut! Quick, while it's gone," she hissed, struggling to maneuver her freed hand to a dry spot. Lut peeked out from behind the rock, then started his dancing bounce between dry patches again, moving toward the tunnel. Away from her.

Mara's heart sank. "No! Lut, please, you have to help me!" He reached the edge of the alcove, checked the direction the monster had gone, and crept into the tunnel.

"Lut," she pleaded. "Don't leave me!"

Lut hesitated, looked back at her, looked ahead at the tunnel. He hissed and snarled and then scrambled back across the dry patches toward her.

"Thank you," she breathed, stretching her free hand toward him. He caught it and pulled, straining until the rest of her arm came free. The clicking seemed to join in with several others. How many of the monsters were here? Her chest tightened in fear, making it hard to breathe.

Lut leaned backwards, putting his whole weight into the task. She wiggled and squirmed. Slowly, fraction by fraction, she came unstuck, leaving behind several strands of hair and gaining a debilitating burning sensation along her scalp and neck.

Now that she could partially sit up, she found a better position to work with Lut and get the rest of her free. She gasped as the last portion of skin lost contact with the gel and promptly blazed with invisible fire, but Lut was already dragging her to her feet and darting back to the tunnel.

They stopped at the edge of the alcove, Mara taking care of where she put her hand. The glowing stones diminished along the tunnel, and it was too dark to see very far. All she could make out were the continuous clicking sounds. Had they gotten louder? She couldn't tell.

Lut tugged at her again, hissing and pulling her the opposite way down the tunnel, away from the noises. She followed, her legs wobbling and threatening to give out on her. She had to hold onto the last vestiges of strength remaining in her body to keep from collapsing in a heap.

Without warning, Lut yanked her sideways. She stumbled to keep from falling over. He hissed some more, and she was startled to feel his hand grip her ankle. He steered her foot, lifting it high and placing it deliberately down a distance away. He repeated the motion with her other foot, and it finally clicked that he was guiding her around an obstacle, perhaps more of the gel.

They set off again, a little slower this time, and she did her best to pay attention to Lut's subtle shifts in direction through the pitch-black tunnel. The exhaustion wore deeper into her bones and joints, fighting to convince her it would be best to just curl up and go to sleep.

It took so much focus to fight off that sense and pay attention to Lut's directions that she almost didn't notice the clicking sound get louder. Lut shrieked and pulled harder, speeding them up. She grunted in pain and struggled to keep her feet moving.

The clicking and brushing sound thundered in her ears. She sensed movement just behind her and let her stagger carry her sideways. A jagged fork of the monster's mandible stabbed through her pack, barely missing her shoulder. The strap caught on the sharp edge, and the monster yanked her backwards, lifting her clear off her feet.

Lut hissed and snarled, pulling on her arm all the harder. The monster tilted its head, raising Mara further from the ground, and she felt the other mandible grasping at her body. She twisted and kicked at the beast as hard as she could. Her first leg only hit and slid off something smooth, perhaps a corner of the shell.

She swung the other one high, aiming for what she thought was just above the mandible holding her captive, hoping to hit its eyes. She hit something that gave under the blow. A terrible grinding noise filled the tunnel as the monster flailed backwards, dragging both Mara and Lut with it.

Mara struggled to reach the jagged appendage keeping her stuck, swinging at the darkness and hoping to find what she was looking for. The second mandible swung closer once more, and she caught it, fighting to push it away. Cold gel slid down a few of her fingers, and she screamed and kicked again. The monster made the horrible sound once more and swung its head violently, slamming her against the wall and sending flashes of light through her vision.

Lut shrieked, his feet scuffing against the rock floor.

Mara clenched the mandible tighter and shoved off the wall with both feet, twisting herself at an angle so her pack slipped free from the appendage that had hooked the strap. She dropped low enough that her toes brushed the floor, but she was still held fast by the gel on her fingers.

The monster reared backwards again, this time at the same moment Lut gave a powerful yank. Her fingers came unstuck, and she tumbled backwards into Lut. He dragged her, trying to pull her up, but her legs wouldn't hold her. Dizziness and nausea gripped her, and it was all she could do to keep from throwing up or passing out. Lut scooped her up and ran, leaping onto the steep slope they'd come from and sliding down it at top speed. The grinding roar and clicking disappeared into blackness behind them.

Chapter 13

M*ikell*

"What if you just used a little bit of your energy to check on her?" Mikell asked, picking his way carefully around some loose stones and uneven patches. The path still worked its way downward, though it wasn't nearly as steep as before.

"That's not how it works. I'm sorry." Ari lightly stepped over mass of grit and gravel.

"How about the Hranites? You could tell where they are, right? Like you could tell there were underdwellers down that other tunnel."

"When did you become so eager for magic use?" Korent asked.

Mikell scowled at the back of his friend's head. "I'm not," he snapped.

"Could've fooled me," Korent snorted, looking over his shoulder.

"Finding Mara, or locating our enemies, is crucial. It would be foolish not to use every resource available to us."

"And you think the best solution is to have Ari stop watching for signs of the stone to drain all her energy trying to do things she can't?"

"She did it before," Mikell retorted. "It's not that unreasonable to assume she could do it again."

"Let me know if my walking is bothering your argument," Ari called back. Mikell realized he and Korent had both stopped. They quickly caught up, placing their feet carefully as they went. A handful of loose rocks skittered from Korent's pace and tumbled over the edge.

Mikell paused, tilting his ear. "Did you hear that?"

"More underdwellers?" Korent asked, his tone hushed and on guard.

"No." Mikell grabbed another pebble and deliberately tossed it over the side, listening intently. An almost inaudible clack of the pebble striking rock reached his ears. "Did you hear it?"

Korent knelt at the edge and waved his torch lower. "We can't be at the bottom already."

Ari similarly crouched at his side. "More likely a wider ledge beneath us."

"Is there any way down there?" Mikell asked. "We could start back in the other direction. You said Mara was more likely that way, didn't you?" He pointed back the opposite way. "This way, we wouldn't be backtracking."

Ari studied the darkness below them. "Perhaps. Though, like I said, those winding tunnels could have us going a completely different direction than we first thought."

"It would be worth checking, wouldn't it?" Mikell asked. He saw a dark look form on Korent's face and elaborated. "I mean, not just for our assurance, but since there's a different path we could be taking IF it's the right direction. Otherwise, we should stay with this one rather than try to climb down and risk falling."

The dark look shifted into a contemplative one. "It's hard to say. You're right about that, and we also know we could run into an unknown number of Hranites or underdwellers."

Both men looked at Ari. She still examined the darkness beneath them, deep in thought. "I should do it."

"You're sure it won't take too much out of you?" Korent asked.

"I'm not sure, but our supplies won't last forever, especially after so many were lost," she replied. "The faster we can find Mara and the stone, the better." She moved away from the edge, sat with her back to the wall, and closed her eyes, remaining still for a while. Then her head tipped back and rested against the wall, and she spoke without opening her eyes, sounding tired. "She's still further down. I can't tell how far, but I don't think she's close."

"And?" Mikell prompted. Korent jabbed him with an elbow.

"It's hard to tell, but I think she's that way." She gestured back the direction they came. "Sort of."

"So we should go down and double back," Mikell interpreted. He returned to the edge and peered over.

"We might try going a bit further on," Korent suggested as he sat beside Ari and dug into his pack. "This path is still sloping downward. Maybe they meet ahead. Or at least get closer, so we don't risk breaking our necks if we fall." He pulled out some dried meat and handed it to the Kadrian.

"All right, let's get going." Mikell turned down the path.

"After a minute to rest," Korent replied. "We can't keep going at top speed—and asking Ari to use more magic than she can spare," he gave Mikell a pointed look, "without stopping to rest every now and then."

"It won't take long," Ari said between bites.

Mikell's stomach grumbled. He dug out some food and took a bite as he resumed walking. "I'll scout ahead, then. If the two paths connect, or if there's an easier spot to climb down from, I'll find it. Otherwise, we'll climb down here." Less wasted time that way. He dug out one of his unlit torches.

Korent stood and brought the torch over to light Mikell's. "It's okay to take a minute to breathe, brother."

"Would you say that if she was the one we lost?" Mikell asked, keeping his voice low and nodding toward Ari.

Korent was silent a moment, then clapped him on the good shoulder. "Be careful. Keep a close watch as you go."

"Quit mothering," Mikell teased. "You might be king of the treeapes, but you're not the king of me."

Korent grinned and gave him a light shove, then returned to sit beside Ari once more.

Mikell walked along the edge of the path, knocking loose rocks over the side every few steps. The lower path seemed just as far away each time, though it was hard to tell for sure. As he got further along, though, the clacking noise came sooner. He tore a corner of cloth off his shirt, lit it from the torch, and tossed it over the edge. The light was barely visible when it stopped. The other ledge was still too far down.

The other two caught up shortly after that. "No luck?" Korent asked.

"It's closer now, but not by much." Mikell eyed the path forward. "It looks like our route gets steep again. Maybe you're right, and they do connect."

"Let's find out, then." Ari sounded less tired now.

Mikell was right that the path dropped into a rather steep slope again, but this time, it vanished into darkness after only twenty paces. Mikell lit another scrap of cloth and tossed it over the abrupt end of their route. Still too far, but they didn't have much choice. "We'll have to climb down. Where's the rope?"

He and Ari examined the slope for a place to attach the rope while Korent dug it out and untangled it from the hasty packing he'd done when they encountered the underdwellers. The only place they found which might be able to hold the rope secure was a jutting rock a few paces from the top of the slope, but didn't look too promising.

Mikell helped tie the rope in place, then leaned back against it, testing to be sure the hold was solid. It shifted a couple fingerlengths as soon as he put his weight on it, and he hastily caught his balance before he fell over backwards. "Perhaps not."

"Let's try another place," Korent suggested.

Mikell gestured. "And where would that be?"

Korent looked around. "Further back along the path?"

"We can check," Ari said. "I'd rather not trust this if we have any alternative. If it moved that much when you merely leaned on it, there's no way it'll hold me."

Faint shuffling sounds caught Mikell's attention. He straightened, looking up, then back the way they'd come, peeking over the edge to the level area. Bobbing lights danced in the darkness, coming straight toward them. "I'm not sure we have a choice," he hissed, crouching back down and gesturing the others' attention toward the coming threat.

"The Hranites?" Korent whispered, staring.

It had to be, as underdwellers wouldn't be using torches, but Mikell didn't want to believe it. There were too many lights. Far too many. Ari and Korent been right in stopping him from revealing their location earlier. And the enemy was already close enough that extinguishing torches and trying to hide wouldn't work. They'd have already seen the light.

"Move fast," Mikell hissed, plunging into action. "Korent, you're going down first and watching for something more secure to attach the rope to. Ari, help me with this end." He knelt beside the weak anchor point, trying to think of some other way to adjust the rope so it would hold their combined weight.

Korent knelt beside him. "This isn't going to work. You're the lightest. You should go first."

"If we can't get this secure, then it won't matter. We'll need all three of us here to fight."

"Then who will find Mara and the stone?" Korent worked the rope over a bulge on the anchor point, managing to snag it underneath. "You have to. At least one of us has to get out of here alive."

Mikell tugged on the rope. It slid a fraction, but held for the moment. "Ari should go."

"What?" both Korent and Ari hissed at the same time.

"You've got the best chance of finding Mara, and the only chance of finding the stone." He hated the words as he said them, but it was the truth. "How close are they?"

Korent straightened to look. Mikell heard a faint whistling sound. "Korent, get down!" He grabbed at his friend a moment too late. The rock hit Korent's forehead with a sickening smack, sending him tumbling down the slope. Mikell lunged, catching Krorent's arm with one hand and the rope with the other. The rope caught and held for a brief moment, but it slipped over the bulge and slid free. Korent dropped over the edge, and Mikell felt himself following. Ari caught the end of the rope and slid a pace before she managed to brace herself against another protrusion, straining against their combined weight.

Mikell's heart pounded in his ears. His body shook under the strain, with his chest caught painfully against the edge of the dropoff. The sharp rock jabbed into his ribs, making it hard to get a full breath. If Korent could find a handhold on the wall beside him, then they both could climb, either up or down. But Korent hung limply from his increasingly sweaty grip. "Korent!" he tried to nudge his friend with his dangling foot. "Korent, wake up!" Korent groaned, but didn't stir.

"Hang on," Ari grunted in a voice drawn tight from exertion. She shifted her feet against the upspurt of rock, all but lying flat on the path for how hard she was leaning to counter the dangling weight on the other end of the rope. She tried to pull them higher, but Mikell could see it was all she could do just to keep them braced from falling any further.

"Well, well." Mundin's tone was smug. He crouched at the top of the slope, looking down on them in mock pity. "Looks like we caught up at just the right moment."

"Foul snake," Mikell managed to spit out.

"We could help you," Mundin shrugged. "It would seem to me you could use some assistance, don't you think?"

As if to agree with him, the rope slid another fingerlength. Ari clenched her teeth, rebracing her feet and struggling to keep her grip. She shot a glare back toward Mundin and the Hranites gathered behind him. "How are you still alive? You found some fools who didn't realize you betrayed them and tried to have them slaughtered?"

A rasping laugh echoed through the Hranites. Mundin grinned. "Of course they know all about it. But betrayal isn't so uncommon in Ebrun as it is in Kenara. And as much as they would have liked to hang me from their parapets—" he glanced back at the Hranites briefly, "and they do have marvelous parapets, if you ever get a chance to see them—but the idea of a stone that could so potently enhance a magic user's abilities... that was something they just couldn't pass up."

"And they didn't kill you the instant you told them where to find it?" Ari grunted, leaning further back in an attempt to strengthen her position.

"He didn't know where to find it," one Hranite snorted in the grating voice so typical of their kind. The speaker might have been female, but it was hard to tell. "He only knew where you would begin looking. And he has more information he refuses to share in order to keep his sorry skin intact."

The rope shifted again. Mikell winced and struggled to breathe as the edge seemed to dig in deeper. Ari met his eyes and glanced toward the wall, seeming to ask if he could reach the side. He nudged at Korent again, still with no result. He gave a tiny head shake. As long as he had to maintain a grip on both the rope and Korent, there was nothing he could do.

"I've only held back a few tidbits," Mundin said cheerfully. "You know, essential information about the stone which I memorized before destroying the pages they were written on."

"You tore the pages out of the journals." Ari strained, trying again to pull Mikell up higher.

"There's only one thing I don't know," Mundin said, "and that's how to locate the stones. You lot hardly seemed to have any solid direction as you wandered into this place, but you must have found some signs pointing you the right way. We couldn't get close enough without being spotted, unfortunately. So tell us what we couldn't glean from eavesdropping. How do you find the stone?"

"Choke and die," Mikell snapped around a cough.

"No, that's what you're about to do," Mundin snorted. "But we could change that. After you tell us what we need to know."

Ari only shook her head.

"I could convince them," the same Hranite said.

"You could, perhaps." Mundin paused, studying their situation. "Though if you do that, I believe the Kadrian will drop the Elves."

"Why would we need them if the Kadrian knows everything we need?"

Mundin turned his attention back to Ari, gesturing toward the Hranite as he spoke. "The lady's right, you know. Last chance to cooperate before losing your Elf friends."

Ari closed her eyes and didn't answer, her forehead scrunched while she pulled at the rope as hard as she could.

"Really? I expected more from you." Mundin shook his head, then gestured to the Hranite beside him. "Proceed."

The Hranite lifted a hand. Nothing happened. Mikell was about to work out a sharp retort when an excruciating pain tore through his wrist so sharply he almost lost his grip on the rope. His ears filled with agonized cries that he only dimly recognized as his and Ari's. He stared in horror as a lump grew underneath his flesh, then cried out again as it began crawling upward, moving beneath his skin with devastating pain with each fraction it climbed.

Ari clenched her teeth, pain and shock in her eyes. Her fingers slipped on the rope, and she barely managed to restore her grip before Mikell's shoulders dropped beneath the edge.

"They're strong," the Hranite said. "Most would have let go by now."

Ari looked at Mikell. The agony made it hard for him to focus and even harder to breathe. The lump under his skin worked its way up his bicep, shredding through sinews and muscle as it went. He managed to shake his head no and hoped, by Maker's favor, she would understand his meaning. Don't give in. Don't give them what they want.

Ari closed her eyes once more, then pushed away from the rock she'd been braced against, sending all three of them tumbling over the edge.

Chapter 14

Mara rested beside the small pool where Lut had brought her, leaning against one of the less jagged sections of cave wall. He shuffled around on the other side of the pool, snarling to himself. The light from the torch she'd wedged between two rocks reflected off the water into bizarre patterns on the darker corners of the secluded area.

Lut scuffed his way over, shoved several chunks of moss at her, and promptly scuffed back as soon as she'd taken it. She recognized it as the same moss he'd brought her before. "Thank you," she said before eagerly digging in. As before, the sweet, tangy taste brought with it a new surge of energy, more with each bite she took.

Lut continued his snarling, wobbling his head from side to side. Mara sat up, feeling stronger after only a portion of the pieces he'd given her. "Thank you, Lut," she said again. "That helped a lot. And thank you for saving me." She knew he couldn't understand her words, but hoped he would understand her tone.

He didn't look her way. In fact, he seemed to go out of his way to avoid looking at her.

She thought back. "Are you upset with me because you didn't want to go into that tunnel to begin with? You knew there was danger there, didn't you, and I didn't listen. I'm sorry."

Lut did the head wobble again and still didn't look at her. She studied him closer as she tried to think of how to convey her apology more clearly. It occurred to her that he didn't actually seem angry with her. His head drooped downward, he shuffled his feet, he avoided looking at her. If he were an Elf or any of the other above-ground people, she would say he looked ashamed. She thought again. "Is this—is this because you almost left me? But you came back and saved me. That's what matters."

His demeanor didn't change. He couldn't understand her.

She thought hard, trying to come up with some way to convey either that she was sorry or that he didn't need to feel guilty. She looked down at the remaining pieces of moss in her hands. An idea slipped through her mind. She took one of the pieces, cupped it in both hands, and walked over to him.

He shuffled a step further away from her, but all she did was sit down and hold out the moss with both hands, the same way he'd done when he first offered her some. Lut kept his back to her, then finally peeked over his shoulder. He eyed her hands and turned his back to her once more. Mara stayed still, waiting. Lut wobbled his head a few more times, then turned around, shrugged, and took the moss. She smiled, glad to see him happy again. He sat down next to her and munched on the moss, and she finished eating beside him.

By the time the moss was gone, she felt as if she'd been resting for days. She looked around, trying to work out the best next move. The large cave room had only the one entrance they'd come in through. When they came here, of course, it had been too dark for her to see. Even if it had been illuminated, she'd been too weak to have much awareness of her surroundings. She would have to start over with figuring out what direction to take.

Closing her eyes, she focused on Mikell's image and was frustrated to once again find nothing but darkness. Either he was badly hurt, or she had the worst timing ever. She exhaled. At least she knew a direction again—still upward and toward the right of her current position.

"Are we ready?" she asked, retrieving the torch and heading toward the tunnel leading back out of the room. Lut ambled to her side, making cheerful snarling noises. She smiled; funny how she could distinguish between the different snarl tones now.

Lut abruptly caught her arm just as a loud hissing noise filled the space around them. Mara froze and raised the torch. Furry bodies covered the floor, ceiling, and walls of the tunnel, the underdwellers stopping their movement toward the cave just as abruptly as she stopped her movement out of it.

Lut pushed her behind himself and snarled at the others as they glared at her with open hostility. Mara's mind raced for possibilities, but none came. There was no escape behind her and nothing she could do to defend herself, especially not against so many of them. Lut was the only one who might be able to get her out of this.

The underdwellers hissed and snarled in angry tones, occasionally gesturing toward her. Lut wobbled his head and danced from one foot to the other as he snarled back. Mara, for her part, did her best to look non-threatening. Lut gestured to his arm. One of the others, a particularly large one, grabbed Lut's arm and sniffed at it a few times. Maybe they would let her pass since she'd helped Lut? She could only hope.

The big one shoved Lut back toward her, gesturing and snarling wildly. Lut took her hand, tugged on it, and pointed to the big underdweller. She took a step forward, and Lut instantly yanked her back to a chorus of threatening hisses.

"Sorry," she gasped. Moving forward wasn't what he wanted, apparently. She looked over the big one, but couldn't figure out what she was supposed to be doing. Lut tugged on her arm and pointed again. "I'm sorry, I don't know what you want." She almost shrugged before remembering that meant something different to them.

Lut snarled under his breath a moment, then tugged her arm emphatically, pointed to his own arm, then to the big one. She stared at Lut's arm. It was the one she'd healed. Did he mean the other underdweller needed healing, too? It wouldn't hurt to check. She slid her hand out of Lut's and turned her palm toward the big one, careful not to extend her hand and make it look like she was reaching for him. As she sent healing to his body, her energy coalesced and centered on the underdweller's shoulder, apparently where the injury was.

The big one snarled and hissed, backpedaling and grabbing at his shoulder much as Lut had when she healed him. She kept at it until the job was done, then lowered her hand, hoping it was enough to convince them not to kill her. The others were already hissing again, obviously alarmed by their leader's reaction.

But the big one stretched his arm upward and moved it around, seeming to marvel at it. He snarled first at Lut, then over his shoulder. The hissing turned into calmer-sounding snarls. Many underdwellers shoved their way through the others to cluster on the floor just behind the big one. Lut shrugged and tugged her hand again before gesturing to the ones that had gathered.

"Oh," Mara said, understanding. "You all need healing, too." She looked over the mass of underdwellers that watched her with expectation in their eyes. Good thing the moss restored so much of her energy. She was going to need it.

Fortunately, most of the injuries were minor, and it wasn't long before she'd finished the task. The underdwellers shrugged and did the funny, arm-waving dance, jabbering excitedly to each other. The big one gave a forceful snarl, quieting the others. He eyed Mara, then shrugged. She relaxed. It had worked.

Lut spoke to the leader for a while, then the underdwellers swarmed past them on the walls and ceiling, leaving Mara briefly dizzy with the sensation of the walls moving around her. Lut tugged her hand onward.

They hadn't been walking long before coming across a tunnel that branched off to the left, and another one further ahead that branched to the right. Mara started toward the further one. Lut quickly caught her hand again and pulled her toward the leftward one.

"But my friends are that way," she said, pointing to the right one. Lut snarled a minute as if explaining something and gestured back toward the other underdwellers before pointing to the tunnel he wanted to go in. Mara opened her mouth to protest, then closed it. Perhaps the underdwellers had seen Mikell and the others. Perhaps they'd told Lut which way to go. She exhaled. It wasn't like she had any idea how to navigate in these caves. And last time she hadn't listened to Lut, they'd nearly been killed. "Okay, Lut. I trust you. Let's go."

Chapter 15

Mikell

The tumble through darkness only lasted for moments before Mikell hit icy water with a splash. His lungs instinctively clenched, and he flailed his arms at the powerful current with little results. The pull of the water thrust his head above surface. He spat water, coughing. Cold air stung his face as the water carried him faster and faster.

"Korent," Ari's voice rasped from somewhere behind him.

He felt splashes hit him from the side and reached out, catching an arm and pulling it closer to him.

The sound of rushing water abruptly amplified and rang around him. They were going through some sort of tunnel.

Korent coughed and clung to Mikell. "What happened?" His voice echoed strangely around the roar of the driving current.

"Hold on," Ari wheezed. "It's almost gone."

Before Mikell could ask what was almost gone, his feet bounced off a solid rock surface, nearly sending him tumbling beneath the water. He wheeled his legs until he had a sense of running along the rock floor, and just in time, as the water dropped to his chest, then his waist. The water no longer buoyed them, and he only hoped whatever surface they ran along lasted, as there was no way in the pitch black to tell if they were heading for safety or another drop-off.

The sound changed once more as he fought for balance; they had left the tunnel behind. Korent dragged beside him, but Mikell managed to keep his friend mostly upright as they staggered and recovered from the sudden shift in momentum. The water continued dropping, the current weakening until it was completely gone.

Mikell let himself fall to his knees. Korent grunted in surprise, dropping beside him. "How about a warning next time, wastik-breath?"

"Figured the king of the treeapes would have better reflexes than that," Mikell shot back. It was a weak retort, but he didn't care. They were all alive. The terrifying *thing* in his arm seemed to be gone. They'd escaped.

"I was going to ask if you two were okay, but I guess that answers that." A light flickered to life in Ari's hand. She leaned against the rock wall beside them, eyes closed, face drained. Korent pulled a torch from his pack and lit it off the fire hovering above her palm, and she dropped her hand, letting the flame stay with the torch. She eyed him. "You're hurt."

Korent gingerly touched the side of his forehead and came away with a bloody hand. "I'll be all right." He dug out some bandages, shoving the torch into Mikell's hand, and she helped him tend to the wound.

Mikell looked back the way the current had carried them, searching for any indication of pursuit. "Are we sure it's safe to make a light?" They were on a wide ledge bordering the cavern, hopefully the same ledge they'd been trying to reach. The rocks glistened from the abrupt bath, and a few trickles of water still washed their way down the slope. He faintly saw the outline of the tunnel they'd gone through.

Ari jerked a thumb back the way they'd come. "The tunnel's long enough that it should keep them from seeing. Besides, we're probably far enough away by now that they wouldn't see much anyway."

Mikell squinted, but of course could see nothing beyond the torchlight. "How far did we come, exactly?"

"Far." The one word carried a hefty weight of exhaustion in her voice. "But at least I managed to keep it on the ledge we were trying to reach."

"Here," Korent handed her some food. "That took a lot out of you."

"Thank you. The water was quite a distance away." She took a bite. "With any hope, they'll think we fell to our deaths. Even if not, it'll take them some time to climb down safely."

Mikell rubbed his arm. Now that he was sure there was no immediate threat from their attackers, he could turn his attention elsewhere. There were no signs of a lump or any damage. His arm still ached, but he wasn't sure if that was from actual injury or just the memory of the horrible pain. "What... that Hranite... what was that?"

Ari rubbed at her own arm, seeming mindless of the action. "A magic attack. Something most can't do, thankfully."

"Magic?" The word tasted foul in his mouth. "You said magic users can't directly affect a person's body."

"Only one group can, but it's rare."

"Which is saying something, because magic users aren't particularly common to begin with," Korent supplied.

"Well?" Mikell demanded, tired of her evasiveness. "What group can do that?"

She eyed him. "Healers."

He stared. "That's—no. That's ridiculous! That wasn't healing. That wasn't anything like healing."

"It's a perversion of a healer's abilities. It's also an arduous undertaking. Very few people know how to do it, and even fewer have the power needed to sustain it."

"But you know how it's done." Mikell didn't bother trying to temper the accusation in his tone.

She laughed, caught herself, and spoke with that vaguely amused expression that was so maddening. "No. The only person I know of in Kenara who can do such a thing is Tashan, and of course she would never use it herself. I imagine it's a hot commodity in Ebrun, which is why I'm glad it's so difficult to learn. Apparently Mundin found a healer with the skill for it."

Mikell shook his head, still unable to believe that anyone with the same skills as Mara, the ability to soothe an ache or mend a wound with a touch, could ever do such a thing. "Not a healer. It can't be."

Ari finished her food and brushed off her hands. "We should move on. It won't be too much longer before they work their way down here."

"But we can rest a moment longer if you need," Korent said, tucking the rope back inside his pack.

She smiled at him, but stood. "We can rest again later. For now, I'd rather put more distance between us and those Hranites."

Mikell took the rear once more, occasionally looking back for signs of bobbing lights dancing after them. The path continued on a gentle slope downward. At least they were going the right direction to find Mara—he hoped. They went as quickly as they could, though Ari's limp had gotten worse.

If Mara was there, the limp would have been gone from the moment it was discovered. And if he hadn't said those harsh things to her, she would have been beside him instead of so far ahead. Mikell steeled himself against the recurring guilt. The instant they found her, he would kiss her, apologize, and do whatever it took to make things right.

Ari stumbled. Korent caught her arm, but she pulled away and ran her hand over the wall, apparently startled rather than hurt.

"What is it?" Korent asked.

"A marker," she breathed, excitement energizing her voice. "It's that same energy that led us here."

"To find the stone?" Mikell moved closer, his eyes drawn to the place her hand rested, though of course it only looked like the same rock as everywhere else around them.

"We're back on the trail?" Korent asked, the same excitement in his tone.

Ari looked the wall up and down, then felt along the wall beyond the marker. Her fingers disappeared into a crack, and she smiled. "We'd have walked right past this," she said, stepping forward and half-disappearing behind what had looked like shadowy crack but was apparently another passageway.

"Good thing you were 'looking,' then," Korent grinned.

She rewarded him with a smile and stepped back, waving him toward the opening. "It's narrow. We'll need the torch at the lead."

Mikell took one last glance backwards before the light disappeared into their new route. Still no signs of the Hranites—good. With any fortune, their pursuers would never detect the narrow passage. He followed the others through the tight space. It wasn't long before a bisecting tunnel hit at a sharp angle, almost back the way they came, and Ari touched another spot on the wall. "This way."

The markers led them on just as convoluted a route as the stone circles had. Mikell's feet and legs protested, but determination helped him ignore their whining chorus. Finding the stone meant Ari would be able to find Mara. And they would keep the dangerous artifact out of the hands of the Hranites.

Eagerness propelled them even faster until they took one sharp turn and found themselves at a dead end. The tunnel they'd walked through widened into a large, circular room, domed high above their heads with a mass of craggy stalactites. There were no signs of any way through.

"You're sure this is where we're supposed to be?" Mikell asked.

Ari stepped back to the main tunnel and placed her hand against the wall. "This has to be it. It's where the markers lead."

Korent walked around the perimeter of the room, sweeping the torch along the walls. "I don't see where we go from here. What do you see?"

Ari slowly walked around the room, her hand hovering just off the surface of the rock. She frowned and took a second walk. Then she stood in the middle of the room, hands extended outward toward the walls on either side and closed her eyes. A long silence passed before she shook her head, looking puzzled and frustrated. "There aren't any other markers here."

Mikell turned around in place, scrutinizing the walls. "But it's empty."

"This has to be the place." Ari frowned around the empty room. "The trail ends here."

"It's been centuries," Korent said. "Perhaps someone already found it."

"I think people would have noticed if a person was suddenly doing far greater magic than feasible." Ari sounded irritated as she walked around the room again, her steps choppy between the limp and her frustration.

"It's possible the underdwellers found it and thought it was pretty enough to hide away somewhere," Korent suggested. "Anything could have happened."

"It has to be here," Mikell said, not caring how desperate he sounded. The stone was their best chance at finding Mara before she was hurt or killed. It was the whole reason they'd risked their lives to begin with. This couldn't have been for nothing. "Maybe it's hidden."

Korent gestured around the bare room. "Where?"

Mikell looked at the relatively smooth walls and floor. "We must be missing something."

Ari slowly waved her hands in the direction of the floor, then up the walls, then across the ceiling. She came to a sudden stop, one hand extended toward the ceiling at the edge of the room. "Oh."

"What?" Mikell peered at the spot, clinging to renewed hope. "Did you find it?"

She walked toward the center of the room, hand still extended. Some of the stalactites seemed to catch glimmers of her movement in reflections of the flickering torchlight.

"What did you find?" Korent asked. "Did they mark one of the stalactites? Are we supposed to climb up?" He raised the torch higher, but there was no sign of any opening above them.

"Not just one." Ari drew a large circle in the air, the center of the circle not quite lining up with the center of the round room.

"Another circle for direction? But the only way out is back the way we came." Mikell took another look around the walls. There had to be something, some clue of where to go next.

"Where's it pointing?" Korent asked.

"I'm not sure." Ari pointed to three different stalactites near the side edge of the room, almost opposite the entrance. "All three of those have a stronger marking than the others. I don't know how to tell which one we're supposed to follow."

"Which three?" Mikell asked, moving closer and peering upward.

"These." Ari pointed to one with a sandy tone and two gray ones with wobbly rings around them. "And this is the circle." She waved her arm again to indicate the broader ring of marked stalactites.

Mikell studied the layout. All three of the marks were along one side of the circle, it appeared, with two of them closer together along the circle than the other. Each showed three completely different directions. And all of those directions pointed straight at solid rock wall.

Korent was already inspecting the wall in one of the indicated directions. "Nothing here."

"Or here," Ari said, running a hand along the wall at the next one.

Mikell glanced at the direction the last mark pointed before returning his focus above. He didn't bother paying attention as Korent inspected the last section of wall and reported his lack of findings once again. The circles always had one stone marked to tell them the direction. The marking system had changed dramatically. "They wouldn't change the way of doing things without a reason. There must be something different this one is telling us."

"Maybe they make an arrow?" Korent suggested, tracing a path in the air from the two outer ones toward the center one. The arrow pointed close to where the middle one alone had indicated, but not exactly.

Ari shook her head as she stepped over and inspected the wall at the new location. "No. Nothing." Frustration bit her words.

"An arrow would still point direction. Why not just mark one if that was the answer?" Mikell stared up at the three points. Then stopped. "Three points... it's not an arrow, it's a triangle."

Korent looked blank. "So what's that mean?"

"Maybe the stone's hiding place is in the center of the triangle. Or halfway between the two further points. If not the stone, then there must be some clue." There had to be. There just had to be.

Ari stood under the center of the triangle. "Korent."

Korent crouched at her side, his hands laced together as a step, and boosted her up. She searched the stalactites with her hands, first the one in the center of the triangle, then the ones along the far line between the two outer points, and then the others contained within the space.

"Well?" Mikell demanded.

"I don't know. None of them seem marked in any way, magic or otherwise." She stretched to reach another. "I don't see any—"

"Woah!" Korent stumbled a pace sideways. "Warn me before you lean like that, if you please."

Ari gripped a stalactite beside her with both hands. "It moved."

"What?" Mikell hurried closer.

She pushed at it again, but it didn't budge. "I grabbed it to keep my balance, and I know I felt it move."

Korent lowered her down. "Boost me."

"I will," Mikell said, stepping forward.

"With your shoulder?" Ari shook her head and laced her fingers for Korent.

Once he was up, he pushed at the same stalactite. "It's loose, somehow, but it's not going far."

"Okay, so what does that mean?" Mikell asked. "How can a stalactite be 'loose,' anyway?"

Korent gestured, and Ari brought him back down. "No idea," he said.

Mikell studied the stalactite in question. It was ruddy, with lines marking the wear of the ages, but didn't look much different from all the others around it. "Do you think we're supposed to break it off?"

Ari's lips quirked in thought. "I suppose... it's possible that whoever hid the stone did have magic ability with rocks, like Tashan does. They could have enclosed the stone in the stalactite and created a way for it to be loose enough to get the attention of whoever knows what they're looking for. Anyone else wouldn't be poking around the ceiling in the first place, I imagine, and even if they did, they would consider a wobbly stalactite to be a hazard rather than a sign."

"Can you sense it? It's a magic thing, right?" Mikell asked.

"I don't sense any magic, but that doesn't mean anything. The rock might be a different sort of magic than what I'm familiar with, or it could have been shielded. For all we know, it might not have magic at all, but simply reflects and enhances what comes into it."

"Okay, so maybe it's inside the stalactite, but you can't work with rocks," Korent said. "So how do we get it down?"

Mikell dug into Korent's pack and found the rope. "Old-fashioned muscle power."

With another boost from Korent, Ari secured the rope around the widest point of the stalactite. The three of them backed up as far as they could to get a strong angle and reduce the chances that the rope would merely slide off the end, then heaved with all their might. At first, nothing happened, but then the rock budged, the stone groaning against their force.

"Harder!" Mikell coaxed, putting his whole weight against his good hand's grip on the rope. The other two dug their feet in and strained.

The rope seemed to vibrate for a moment, as if registering a complaint. The stalactite broke free, sending them tumbling backwards as it crashed to the floor. It shattered, pieces scattering everywhere. Mikell grunted first as he hit the floor, then a second time as a fist-sized chunk of rock smacked into his leg.

Ari sat up, rubbing at her elbow. She began to say something, but came to a stop, eyes fixed on the floor beyond them.

Mikell turned to see what she was looking at and spotted it. In the middle of the broken stalactite pieces was a rough green stone the size of Mikell's head. It took him a moment to find his voice. "Is that it? That has to be it, right?"

Ari was already on her feet and crossing to the stone. She picked it up, and her eyes lit with wonder. "This is it."

Korent let out a whoop and caught her around the waist in a quick spin of victory.

Mikell took a step closer as the twirl came to an end, staring at the almost hypnotic swirls of green covering the stone. "Is it—does it do what the writings say?" His heart thumped against his chest. They finally found it, and now they would find Mara.

Ari disentangled herself from Korent's grip and held the stone in front of her. A smile twitched at the corners of her mouth. "It's... amazing." Mikell felt warmth rush through him, and his shoulder, his legs, all his aches and pains were better. Korent and Ari both looked similarly better, bruises and gashes gone. A ball of fire sprang to life in the center of the space, large but comfortably warm. "It hardly takes anything to work. I could keep us warm all the way back out of this mountain. I could draw up clean water from anywhere, no matter how far away."

"And Mara?" Mikell pressed impatiently.

Ari focused on the rock, then turned, nodding toward the far end of the room opposite the tunnel. "She's that way, and downward a ways. I can see her. She's... she looks like she's been through a lot, but she's okay." Ari's brow crinkled. "It seems like someone's leading her, but I can't make it out."

"Leading her?" Mikell frowned. Who else was down here except for underdwellers and Hranites? "How do we get to her?"

Ari tipped her head, still staring at the rock. "Huh. I wonder..." She focused once again. The ground seemed to rumble for a moment, then the wall at the far end of the room seemed to shift and swirl, spinning faster as it opened into a round tunnel leading downward at a moderate angle. The other end came to a stop, and a cry of surprise echoed back up the passage.

Mikell's breath caught as he recognized the voice. "Mara?" He leaned on the edge of the tunnel, peering down into the darkness. "Mara!"

"Mikell!" Her voice was faint at the distant end of the tunnel, but a light flashed into view, and he could see her face looking up at him in wonder. She dashed into the tunnel, rushing her way up toward them.

"Ari? What's wrong?" Korent asked.

Mikell was about to jump into the tunnel and all but slide his way down to Mara, but a sharp pain hit him in the chest, stopping him short. He caught the wall for support and took a deep breath to brush away the unexpected pain, but it dug in deeper, as if someone was slowly driving a knife between his ribs.

Adrenaline shot through his system. That magic-user Hranite had found them and was attacking again.

He spun, but it was still only him, Korent, and Ari in the cave. Korent clutched his own chest in pain. Ari had gone completely still, like carved alabaster, her face blank and her eyes fixed on the stone. The stone itself seemed to glow faintly, mixing with the light from the ball of flames in bizarre patterns. His breath caught as the pain drove further. The attack was coming from the stone, or Ari, or both.

"Ari," Korent called again, reaching to shake her. The instant his hand neared her shoulder, a flash of light burst from the stone. Korent flew backwards as if thrown and slammed into the wall.

The blade dug deeper still, and Mikell had to catch the wall to keep from falling over. "Ari! Stop!" She gave no sign she heard. He couldn't even tell if she was breathing.

"Mikell! What's wrong?" Mara called from down the tunnel, hurrying her pace.

She wasn't affected by whatever was attacking them. He had to keep it that way. He stumbled until he was facing her again. "Don't come closer!"

He saw movement in a flash of her torch. An underdweller ran behind Mara, chasing her up the tunnel. A fresh jolt of panic shot through him. "Look out!" He staggered back into the opening, fumbling for his sword. He had to protect his wife from the murderous little beast. The pain drove deeper, making it hard to breathe, and he doubled over.

"Ari, please!" Korent wheezed. He staggered closer to Ari once more. "Listen to me. You have to make this stop. I know you can!"

Mikell glanced back at them, frantic for the pain to end so he could save his wife. Some sort of dark shadow pooled into Ari's fixed eyes. "Make it stop!" he shouted.

Mara gasped in sudden pain, dropping to her knees. The attack had reached her, and now the underdweller was even closer to her, snarling wildly. "Get back!" Mikell managed to shout through the agony crushing his chest.

"Ari!" Korent shouted even louder, his voice just as strained as Mikell's. "Fight it!"

Ari gasped. The stone tumbled from her hands and rolled across the floor as she dropped backwards. The ball of fire vanished, leaving only the flickering light from the torch Korent had dropped and a matching flicker from Mara's torch in the tunnel.

Ari scrambled until her back was against the wall. Still, her feet churned as if trying to get even further from the stone. "Don't touch it!" she screamed, her eyes wide in absolute terror.

The pain vanished, leaving gripping fear behind. Mikell had seen Ari worried, alarmed, even shaken at one point, but he'd never seen her truly frightened. The idea that this thing terrified her was in itself terrifying. He let the fear join with anger and fuel his movement, charging at the underdweller to drive it away from Mara.

The beast hissed and lunged to meet him.

"Ari? Talk to me," Korent pleaded.

"No, stop," Mara shouted. "He's not going to hurt us!"

"Don't touch it!" Ari screamed over and over.

"Lut, don't! These are my friends," Mara cried.

"Ari!" Korent's voice grew sharper.

"Get away from her!" Mikell yelled, raising his sword to strike.

"STOP!" Korent's thundering voice all but shook the cave and tunnel. Mikell stumbled to a halt, sword poised to lob the creature's head off its shoulders, but even the underdweller froze at the commanding tone.

Korent looked down the tunnel, his own sword in hand. His voice was calmer than his tense form would indicate, and it was backed with steely authority. "Mara, is that thing going to hurt you?"

"No. He's been helping me," she quickly explained. "He isn't going to hurt anyone."

"Mikell, put the sword away." Mikell lowered his sword, and Korent turned back to Ari, his voice still strong with authority but tenser than before. "Ari? Answer me. Are you okay?"

Ari only trembled, her eyes darting, unfocused. The darkness still shadowed her narrow green irises.

Mara hurried past Mikell and knelt in front of Ari, reaching out to take the Kadrian's hands. Ari's eyes finally focused on Mara's. They held gaze for a moment, then both women closed their eyes and lowered their heads in concentration.

Mikell kept his sword in hand as he moved closer to the two of them, part of him wanting to grab Mara and pull her away. Who knew what that stone had done to Ari, or what it would cause her to do to Mara?

Korent stepped to his side as if seeing his desire and preparing to intercept. The underdweller skittered up the side of the wall, watching with a curious tilt to its head.

Finally, Ari's trembling stopped. Her shoulders slumped. She opened her eyes, now clear of the darkness, and pushed her hair out of her face with a shaky hand. Mara stood, looking disturbed.

Mikell checked the underdweller, saw he hadn't moved, and hurried to throw his arms around his wife. She melted into his chest, clutching him tight. Korent knelt beside Ari and took her hand. She leaned against him, closing her eyes.

No one spoke for a long time. The underdweller snarled, the sound coming from directly above. He stared down at them from the ceiling. "Nahnah."

Mara giggled, and the tension broke. Mikell drew a deep breath into lungs he hadn't realized were constricted. Mara kept her tight hold on him, but gestured to the underdweller. "This is Lut. He..." She paused, smiled, then straightened her face and continued. "He and I have been through a lot. He's a friend." Then she looked up at Lut and pointed to the others one at a time. "Mikell. Korent. Ari."

"Nih-deh. Doh-nep. Ah-nee."

"That's probably as close as he's going to get," Mara said. She reached up and smoothed Mikell's hair. "Are you all right, tabe-me?"

He looked down at her scraped, bruised, and smudged face. "I'm fine, raisa-me. I'm more worried about you."

She rested against his chest once more. "I'm fine, too."

Lut dropped to the ground and walked around the two of them a few times, occasionally sniffing in Mikell's direction.

Korent took Ari's shoulders and studied her face. "You're all right now?"

She still looked shaken, but more composed. She nodded.

Mikell glanced back at the stone, lying innocently against the opposite wall. "What happened?" he asked. "What was that?"

Ari closed her eyes and shuddered. "There's something in there. Something dark."

The silence stretched before Mikell broke it. "Go on."

She didn't answer for a long time. "I believe I know where the idea came from that magic is inherently evil and corrupts those that use it." She took a deep breath. "It was thrilling. Everything I had done before, I could do with ease, with hardly any effort. I felt even stronger with everything I did, rather than feeling my energy draining like usual. It was... potent."

She closed her eyes. "And then I felt the urge to do something I'd never been able to do before. I can't shape rock the way Tashan does, though I've tried to do it in the past. It seemed the best choice, to create a tunnel so we could reach Mara faster. But as soon as I did it..." She shook her head and shuddered again.

Korent drew her closer. "You're safe now. We all are."

"It took more energy for me to do that. And that somehow opened a way for it to..." She searched for words. "It took over. I didn't know what was happening. That is, I knew in a sense, I could see it, but it was all too distant to seem real." She looked away, clearly disturbed.

"But you fought it," Korent said. "You managed to beat it."

She met his eyes. "I heard you. It was faint, but I could hear your voice calling to me. It was as if I woke up and realized it was *real*, that this thing was using me to attack all of you." She drew in a shaky breath, seeming steadier now. "I fought it and was able to break my grip on the stone, which ended the connection. But there was still something there, like a part of itself left behind. I almost couldn't keep it back and prevent it from taking control again. Mara was able to help me destroy it."

Mikell squeezed his wife tighter. "So it's gone now?"

"Only the part that remained with me." Ari's eyes flickered to the stone. "The rest..."

Korent stood and started toward the stone.

"Don't—" Ari started to shrill, but caught herself and spoke in a more controlled tone. "Don't touch it."

"I think we got that message," Korent said, crouching a safe distance away and examining it.

Ari stood. "What's the thickest material we have?"

"The leather on the packs," Mikell said.

"What else?"

"The blankets are thin, but can be thick if folded," Mara suggested.

"Good. Do that. As thick as possible. Use it to pick up and wrap the stone so the whole thing's covered." Ari dug into her own pack and pulled out her blanket. "Use this one, too."

Korent followed her directions. "So what are we going to do with it? We can't use it."

"And we can't let anyone else use it, either," Ari said. "That... *thing*... wanted to kill everything it came across. I don't think it would have ever stopped." She shook her head as if clearing away the thought. "We have to destroy it."

"How?" Mikell asked.

"Tashan will know. Either she'll find a way to destroy the thing inside, or destroy it all, the thing and the stone together." Ari eyed the wrapping job Korent had done. "Put it in the bottom of your pack, underneath everything else, with any folds turned downward so you don't accidentally reach through and touch it." She hesitated, then crossed the room and crouched beside Korent, speaking quietly to him as he worked.

Lut skittered up the wall again and hovered, watching with curiosity as Ari and Korent worked.

Mikell saw the chance and seized it. "Forgive me," he said softly at the exact same moment Mara said the same. He paused, surprised.

She gave a light smile before speaking seriously again. "I'm sorry. I shouldn't have snapped at you like I did."

"I shouldn't have yelled at you," he replied. "You were right—you saved Korent's life. I should have been proud of you instead of angry. I let my worry for you get the better of me."

"But I should have been more understanding," Mara said. "It's always been your duty to watch out for me."

"Well, I shouldn't have treated you like you weren't capable."

Mara paused, then started laughing.

He joined her and pulled her close. "I was so afraid I'd lost you."

"I felt the same," she whispered into his chest.

"It's set," Korent said, straightening and slinging his bag on his back. "Which way now?"

"Can we follow the markers back to the exit?" Mikell asked.

"Except most of that path crumbled away," Ari reminded him. "We'd get to that area and have no way across."

"Lut might be able to help," Mara offered.

Mikell eyed the underdweller in distaste. He wouldn't attack it for Mara's sake, but that didn't mean he trusted it for a moment.

"Though," Mara continued, "to be honest, I'd rather take some time to rest. It's been…" Her fingers lightly toyed with a torn spot on her shoulder strap, "a lot."

"I would appreciate the rest, myself," Ari said.

"That would probably be best," Korent agreed, rubbing the back of his head. "We can sleep here and decide which way to go after we've all recovered our strength."

"I'm sorry!" Mara reached for Korent. "I forgot you were hurt."

He shook his head, gently deflecting her hand. "It's only a bruise. Nothing that won't be mended with a good rest."

"Then I'll take first watch," Mikell said, sitting down with his back to the wall. He dug out his blanket, and seeing Mara pull out her own, tossed his to Ari. "Since yours is busy insulating the stone."

She looked surprised, but only for a moment. "Thank you."

Mara sat next to Mikell and nestled under his arm, her blanket wrapped around her. "What happened to you? I kept trying to find you, but it was always so dark."

He hesitated, not wanting to worry her. "We ran into some of his kind," he nodded to where Lut was bouncing between stalactites on the ceiling, "and had to hide more than once."

"And we discovered we're not the only ones looking for the stone," Ari said as she sat nearby. "There's a group of Hranites here, led by Mundin."

Mara's eyes widened. "Mundin? How is that possible?"

"It shouldn't be," Mikell agreed. "But apparently he promised to help them find the stone, but won't tell them everything he knows about it so he has something to hold over their heads."

"One of the Hranites is a magic user," Ari said. "A very dangerous magic user."

Mikell felt an involuntary shudder. "She attacked us. It was like there was something under my skin, crawling up my arm."

Mara's face turned pale, and she rubbed her own arm. "Tashan told me about that sort of thing, just before we left."

Interest sparked in Ari's eyes. "Did she teach you how to counter it?"

Mara nodded.

"Good," Ari said. "I'm not skilled enough in healing to fight it myself. Though with any hope, we'll make it out of this mountain without running into them again."

"With any hope," Korent agreed.

"What about you?" Mikell asked, pulling his wife closer. "What happened to you?"

Mara glanced at Lut. "I... I found Lut, and he was injured." She seemed to be choosing her words carefully, like there was something she didn't want to say. "I healed him, and he befriended me."

"I'm amazed he didn't attack you on sight," Ari commented. "The ones we ran into were quite hostile."

A look of discomfort crossed Mara's face, and she avoided eye contact.

Korent leaned forward. "He did attack you."

"He... I think they consider anyone in these tunnels a threat, like a trongial protecting its den. But then I healed him, and he's been my friend here ever since." She looked at Mikell as if uncertain how he'd respond. "He even saved me. There was a..." She stopped, then looked down.

"What?" Mikell asked. She seemed bothered and reluctant to share, and that worried him. What had been so awful she couldn't talk about it?

"We came across some things. They were a bit like pedes, but enormous. Like I said, Lut saved me. He helped me get away."

"Giant pedes?" Korent asked.

Mara nodded. "And they have some sort of sticky goo they use to trap prey."

The thought of his wife facing so much without him to protect her left Mikell simultaneously angry and sick to his stomach. He squeezed her as tight against him as he dared. "I'm glad you're all right."

She gave him a little smile. "I'm glad you're all right, too."

Mikell glanced over at the others. Ari was already yawning and nestling down to rest. Korent lay a respectful distance from her, but close enough to protect if the situation called for it. "Sleep. We'll move on when everyone's rested."

She kissed him, then waved toward the ceiling. "Lut!" She pressed her hands together under her tilted head as if sleeping. The underdweller made a repeated hissing noise.

Mikell tensed at the threatening sound, but Mara pressed a hand on his arm. "It's okay. I'm pretty sure that's how he laughs."

Lut skittered down, turned around a few times, and curled up in a ball where the floor met the wall. Mikell eyed him a bit longer, then relaxed, one hand still resting on his wife as she nestled down to sleep. They'd found her, by Maker's favor. And they'd found the stone. Now they were just going to have to try to get out of there without getting caught by the Hranites. Or the underdwellers. Or those insectoid monsters Mara had described.

This was going to be a challenge.

Chapter 16

Mara woke to find her husband curled close to her, asleep. A fresh sense of relief flooded her at the sight. She'd almost lost hope of finding him before that tunnel opened up in the rock.

Korent sat on watch, one hand tracing patterns on the rock floor and the other resting on Ari's shoulder. He looked Mara's way as she sat up. "We can wake the others."

"No need. Let them rest." She dug out her waterskin and drank. "What did Mikell leave out? I know he was trying to shield me from the worst of it."

Korent chuckled lightly. "You certainly have gotten bolder than when I first met you."

Mara blinked. She didn't feel any bolder than she had before.

Korent continued before she said anything. "He skipped over a few details, I suppose. We had to work our way underwater at one point, as the cave we landed in had no exit except through a stream, and fighting through narrow squeezes underwater—in the dark, no less—wasn't exactly fun. I don't know many of the details of what happened with the Hranites." He lightly touched his forehead. "One of them got me with a sling, I think."

"You don't look too bad for all of that," Mara said, looking him over. She'd expected to find bloody gashes, bruises, possibly even some broken bones.

His hand moved from the patterns on the rock to rest on the pack beside him for a moment. "One of the first things Ari did when she got her hands on that rock was patch us all up."

Mara eyed the pack. The staggering pain digging into her chest and the cold darkness she'd found lurking inside Ari still haunted her mind.

"So," Korent said, returning to the patterns, "what about you? What did you leave out?"

"Me?"

"Yes, you. We could all tell you were holding something back."

She looked down. "It wasn't... I just... Mikell gets so upset when he thinks I've been in danger."

"You're right. And you should still tell him anyway."

"Tell me what?" Mikell sat up beside her, sleep still drooping his eyes.

Ari stirred. "Five more minutes," she mumbled into her arm.

Mara glanced at Korent. He raised an eyebrow and waited. He wasn't going to answer Mikell's question. It was on her to choose how to respond. "I... there was one other thing about the bug monster."

Korent nudged Ari, and she sat, blinking hard and pushing the sleep from her eyes.

Mara looked at her hands. "I got stuck in some of that goo, and it got to us before I could get free. It had some sort of sting that knocked us out and weakened us."

Mikell drew in a sharp intake of breath and took her hands. "You're all right now?"

"Yes, I'm fine. I was able to distract the creature, and Lut helped me get free."

He glanced around the cave room until he spotted Lut braced between two stalactites, digging at the rock ceiling. "I'm glad you had help." His grip tightened. "I should have been there to protect you."

"I'm fine," Mara repeated, trying to reassure him. Part of her wanted to be annoyed, but she knew he meant well. It was just his way of being protective. "We were able to fight it off and escape."

"Fight it off?" Mikell stared at her.

Oops. Maybe she had said too much in trying to reassure him. "I... It almost caught me, but we managed to get away."

"Without any weapons?" Korent sounded impressed.

"I think I kicked it in the eyes." Mara tried to temper the pride in her voice and wasn't sure she succeeded.

Ari laughed. "Good for you."

Mikell was still frowning. "You shouldn't have been put in a situation like that."

"But I was." The words came out harsher than she intended, and she took a breath to quiet her tone, pressing a hand against the side of his face. "It wasn't anyone's fault. We were separated by poor fortune, and we had to find a way to make it through until we could get back to each other. And I managed it well enough. I'm still here, in one piece, after all."

He stared at her a long moment, then looked away.

"We should get going," Ari said, digging through her pack. She frowned and dug deeper.

"What's wrong?" Korent asked.

"I don't have much food and water left in here. How are your supplies?"

The others checked their own packs. Mara and Mikell had hardly any food and only a couple of waterskins between them. Korent and Ari's supplies were low. "We'll have to ration," Ari said. "We don't know how long it'll take before we get out of here."

Mara thought for a moment. "Korent mentioned you had to go through a stream at one point. Have you found many water sources down here?"

"Some, on occasion. They're few and far between, though." Ari got a distant look with a small chuckle as if remembering something. "I just about wiped myself out drawing up enough to catch us when the Hranites attacked."

"But there is water to be found," Mara pressed. Ari nodded. "Then I think we'll be okay. There's something we can eat here," Mara said, looking around. No signs of the moss that she could see, but Lut might know how to find some nearby. "Lut!" He looked down at her, and she made the eating motion. He snarled cheerfully and bounced between the stalactites.

"I'm not eating that thing." Korent eyed the underdweller, but he had a teasing twist to his lips.

Mara couldn't help but giggle as she rolled her eyes. "Not him, silly."

Lut skittered down the wall and deposited a mass of moss in her lap, then shrugged, did his happy dance, and crawled back up to the ceiling. Mara distributed the moss to the others. "Try it. It's delicious." She glanced at Ari. "And refreshing."

The Kadrian nodded in understanding and started to bite, but recoiled at the smell. She looked at Mara with a raised eyebrow.

"Trust me. It's good."

Ari eyed the moss a moment longer, then took a bite, promptly making an exclamation of surprised delight. "It's amazing."

Korent cautiously tasted his with a similar response.

Mikell eyed the green mass in his hands in clear distaste. Mara waited, but he said nothing, to her surprise. She took a bite of her own and put a hand on his arm. "It's safe to eat, I promise."

He stared at the moss a moment longer, then seemed to shake himself as if chasing away some unpleasant thought. "I trust you." He took a bite, chewed slower for a moment, then scarfed down the rest of his portion.

Once they'd seen to their needs, Mara waved to Lut once more, beckoning him down from the ceiling. He dropped to her side, a chunk of moss still hanging out of the side of his mouth. "Lut," she said carefully, trying to think of how best to communicate the request. "We," she gestured to all of them, "need to get out," she pointed upward, "of the mountain," she made a downward angle with her hands. "Can you help us?"

Lut stared blankly, then made his hissing laugh.

Mara sighed and tried again. "We need to find," hand to her forehead as if searching, "a way out," she traced an arcing path with her finger.

Lut shrugged and jabbered.

"I get the impression he has no idea what you're saying," Ari observed.

"I'm afraid not. We've managed to communicate a little, but not very well."

Korent looked at her with a smile. "You'll find a way."

She had a feeling he wasn't referring to Lut.

"We'll have to find our own way out." Mikell looked back at the tunnel opening opposite the one Ari had made, which must have been the way they had come into the room in the first place. "We should retrace the path made by the markers. I know it goes to the collapsed ledge, but if we can get close enough, perhaps we can see another way to reach the exit."

"It's as good a plan as any," Korent agreed.

"I guess I'm leading, then." Ari brushed herself off. She took them through a maze of narrow tunnels before they reached an almost impossibly tight section.

Mikell took the torch and moved ahead. "Stay put. I'll make sure it's clear." Mara watched him squeeze through, then looked at Ari for explanation.

"Last we came this way, the Hranites weren't far behind us," Ari said. "While I would hope they moved on to keep searching, it's possible they chose to wait instead, or leave a few of their numbers behind to watch for us."

"Hopefully not," Korent supplied. "They don't necessarily know we went this way, and even if they did, there could be another way out, for all they know."

"Still, caution is prudent." Ari pushed a chunk of red hair out of her face, then had to do it a second time as it fell right back into its former position.

The light reappeared, followed shortly by Mikell. "It's clear. Let's go."

They squeezed through the narrow tunnel and came out onto a relatively wide path leading left and right, with more rock wall behind them and nothing in front of them but blackness. The same massive cavern, Mara reasoned. The path they stood on angled upwards, and she took a step that direction.

"This way," Ari corrected, taking the light and turning to the downward slope.

"But I thought the way out would be above us."

"It is," Ari said, already walking on, "but the energy markers lead this way. I'm sure the trail will lead upwards again eventually."

"We should stay quiet." Mikell kept his voice low. "We don't want to be caught for talking too loudly."

Lut skittered past on the wall, and Mikell tensed, briefly reaching for his sword before he seemed to remember their new traveling companion. He blew out an annoyed breath. Mara caught his hand and gave it a little squeeze. It had to be hard for her husband to travel with a creature he only knew as a threat.

The trail continued downward, then upward, then downward again before leading into a tunnel driving gently upwards through the rock. Mara's steps lightened with hope. Upward was good. Maybe they'd find the exit soon and be out of the cave before the Hranites found them.

But the hope faded as the hours stretched on, and her legs ached from the continuous march through the unbranching route. The trail zigzagged, sometimes level, sometimes downward, usually upward. They found a trickling waterfall and refreshed themselves. They passed through a large cavern with a ceiling that reflected the light like millions of stars dancing above them. But still no sign they were any closer to the exit than when they'd started.

Lut's good spirits remained, and he was the only one among them not trudging and dragging. He spiraled his way from floor to ceiling to walls, taking particular delight in the room with the reflective ceiling. His cheerfulness and enjoyment of the trek seemed to annoy Mikell all the more. Mara made sure to keep a hold on her husband's hand, doing her best to offer him some support to balance out the annoyance.

"Does it have to keep running all over the walls and ceiling?" Mikell finally grunted.

"Probably not, but this is his home," Mara said as gently as she could. "I think he finds this walk enjoyable."

Mikell muttered something unintelligible.

"I agree," Korent said, a teasing note to his voice. "Nothing gets me more upset than seeing someone else happy."

Mikell gave him a look. "Wastik-breath."

"Snitface."

"Mighty king of the treeapes."

"Slipgrub."

They entered another large cavern, one of the biggest they'd found. Ari stretched the torch upward, but the ceiling, if any, was too high for the light to reach. Another tunnel opening sat on the far end of the room, and a narrow ramp sloped upward along the edge of the wall to their right. The high end of the ramp disappeared into darkness above them while the low end rested at the other end of the cavern by the new tunnel ahead.

Korent peered up at the ramp, craning his neck to see the ledge high above them. "That way, I'm guessing?"

Ari walked slowly around the bottom of the ramp, then faced the tunnel exit instead. "No. It's this way."

"Maybe here's the point to depart from the original trail," Korent suggested. "We already know we're going to reach an impassible area going that way. We might find a different path to the exit if we go this way."

Ari considered the idea, then raised an eyebrow toward Mikell and Mara. "Could be. What do you think?"

Mikell eyed the tunnel, still several paces from them, then the ramp. Lut scampered up the side of the ramp, across the ledge, and up the wall beyond. Mikell jumped at the sudden movement past him, then scowled. "We should try it. The sooner we can get out of here, the better."

Lut snarled cheerfully and crawled the wall beside them as they ascended, his continuous vocalizations seeming to add to Mikell's displeasure. Mara found it strangely comforting, after all that time with only his jabber to listen to. She squeezed Mikell's arm and spoke quietly, so only he could hear. "He's not going to hurt us."

"He's not much help, either," Mikell grunted.

"He was to me."

He looked surprised, then cross, and then he exhaled. "I'm glad he was there to help you, but you're back with us now. I'm not sure we really need him following along."

"What does it hurt?"

His cross look returned, then he once again drew in a slow breath and let it out. "He's a bother. But if it means that much to you for him to stay with us, then I'll try not to let him get to me."

She hadn't expected him to relent so quickly. Pleased, she squeezed his arm tighter. "Thank you."

A sound caught her ear. Mikell froze beside her, apparently hearing the same thing. "Shh!"

Ari and Korent stopped, looking back at the two of them.

A faint glow of light stretched from the tunnel near the end of the ramp. Mikell grabbed his sword. "The Hranites!"

"Put the torch out," Korent hissed. "Move!"

Mikell pushed Mara further up the ramp, staying protectively behind her as they hurried to climb higher in the darkness, each keeping a hand on the wall beside them to avoid losing their direction and falling off the edge. They hadn't been able to see the top of the ramp when they came in. With any fortune, the Hranites wouldn't be able to see it, either.

Mara glanced back over her shoulder. The light was brighter now, and she could hear grating voices echoing their way. She sent a desperate prayer to the Maker that they would find a tunnel, or stay hidden, or anything that would let them get out of this alive.

She almost ran into Korent's back and reeled to a stop, panting. "What's wrong?"

"There's no exit up here," Ari whispered back.

"Get low." Mikell's voice was barely audible. "Keep still."

Mara crouched, huddling tightly against the wall. Lut grabbed her shoulder. She almost jumped out of her shoes and had to clench her teeth together to hold back a yelp of surprise. He snarled, and she pulled at his arm, shaking her head and putting a hand over her mouth. She knew he could see her gestures in the dark; she only hoped he would understand them. He slid down the wall and hunkered next to her, thankfully quiet.

The Hranites entered the room with a blaze of light from their numerous torches, grunting amongst themselves in their guttural language. Mara held her breath against the rush of memories flooding back at the sound. Held at knifepoint, captured, crawling her way through a fight... She closed her eyes and forced herself to draw in slow breaths, as quietly as possible. The Hranites would pass through the cavern. They wouldn't spot where she and her friends hid. It would be okay. She tried to keep her eyes shut but couldn't bear the tension of not knowing if the Hranites were passing by or staring up at them.

Mundin slowed, forcing a bumping, shuffling stop from the Hranites behind him. He jerked a thumb toward the ramp. "You're sure that led nowhere."

"Yes, we're sure," a Hranite woman beside him hissed. "We have already checked twice. You want to check it again, do so yourself."

He glared at the Hranite. "Don't be insolent."

"This is not being insolent. This is being snide. Insolence would be telling you what a grubfaced, pathetic little man you are."

Harsh rumbles filled the cavern. Mara clenched her hands over her ears, and it took her a moment to realize the Hranites were laughing.

Mundin's glare intensified as he resumed his faster pace, his movements sharper with irritation. "It certainly wasn't I who lost them."

"No, you're the one who miscalculated how they would respond to harm and is still unaware of how to find the stone."

A loud grunt came from further back in the mass. Mara's heart froze at the sight of several Hranites looking up the ramp, and she ducked her head even lower, cutting off her view. Ari's single torch in the cavern hadn't been enough to illuminate the top of the ledge, but the numerous torches here spread enough light to all but fill the place. The only thing keeping her and the others out of sight was their low position against the wall, keeping the ramp edge angled between them and the Hranites.

"What is it?" the Hranite leader asked.

The others answered in their own language.

"What?" Mundin snapped.

"They say they saw something move," the leader said.

Feet shuffled around. Mara's heart pounded in her throat. Were they coming up the ramp? Moving to get a better view?

"Probably one of those cave-crawlers," Mundin grunted irritably.

Mara clenched her eyes shut. She couldn't see Mundin, but she could visualize him. *Just a cave-crawler.* She sent the thoughts his direction with all her will powering them onward. *Nothing to waste time on. The stone is more important.*

The leader barked something out in the Hranite language, then spoke to Mundin again. "They will check and see."

No. We need to move on. The stone is more important.

Mundin muttered something under his breath. "Fine, but be quick about it. The stone is more important than a couple of cave-crawlers."

Mara's stomach dropped. She'd failed yet again. Mikell beside her tensed, shifting his feet almost imperceptibly, getting into a better position to leap into attack stance.

Mara's mind raced. There had to be some way to get out of here unseen, or to prevent the Hranites from spotting them. But the lights already advanced on the ramp, drawing closer.

A faint sound came from the tunnel they'd originally come through, like pebbles had been dislodged. "What was that?" Mundin demanded, stepping closer to the tunnel and raising his torch.

"We'll find out when we move on," the Hranite leader said, then barked something in her guttural language. The tone suggested impatience, like she was ordering the others to hurry up with their investigation of the ramp.

Mara clenched her eyes and tried once more to reach Mundin. *They're more likely down this way. Why would they hide on a dead-end ramp? That sound must have been them. They're close. We have to catch them before they get away.*

A startled exclamation interrupted her thoughts. She was too late. The light had reached them.

"It's them!" the leader yelled as the scouts drew their weapons, slowing but keeping the ramp fully blocked.

Mikell jumped to his feet, sword at the ready. Korent rushed past Mara to stand at his sword-brother's side. Lut hissed and snarled before darting up the wall. He vanished into a crack just large enough for his squat body to wriggle through.

"Coward!" Mikell shouted, but the underdweller was already gone.

Mara backed herself into the corner, out of the way of the fighters. Her heart vacillated between betrayal and understanding. They were clearly outnumbered. If there was a way for Lut to escape, then he should take it. Still, his rapid abandonment stung after all they'd been through together.

"And you wanted to just keep going," Mundin sneered at the Hranite leader before addressing the group at the top of the ramp. "How fortunate to find you again. And I do believe you won't find it so easy to weasel away this time."

"Plan?" Ari whispered to the men. Neither of them answered, apparently as much at a loss as she was. Mara stared down at the sea of Hranites beneath them. There was no way to get through, no way to get out.

"So come now," Mundin continued, "I give my word we will leave you unharmed if you tell us how to find the stone."

"Your word doesn't exactly get you far after what you've done," Ari retorted.

"Then let's make it easy," the Hranite leader said, stepping forward and raising her hands.

Mara sensed Mikell and Ari tensing, and she wasn't sure why. A sting caught her wrist and turned into a searing pain. She screamed, looking frantically for the wound. A bulge beneath her skin crawled its way upward, drawing another scream, this one of terror along with the pain.

She fought against the panic, trying to force her thoughts clear. She knew what this was. She knew how to stop it, if she could only focus. The bulge reached her elbow. She clenched her teeth and wrapped her other hand around her bicep, struggling through the pain to focus on what needed to be done.

Her energy finally obeyed the pain-muddled directions, and the wall slid into place. The bulge vanished along with the pain. Now that her screams had ended, she could hear the pained cries from her friends. She spun to them, searching for the attack's location. She couldn't see it through Ari's long sleeves. Couldn't see it on Korent. Spotted it almost at Mikell's shoulder.

Panic twined with her energy, fueled by desperation. She unleashed it in a blast, focusing as hard as she could on the sense of a wall at their shoulders. The others staggered, gasping in relief as the pain ended.

Mara felt another wall, the actual cave wall, hitting her from behind. The world took a spin. She sucked in air, trying to recover her sense of awareness after the massive expenditure of energy.

"Ooh," the Hranite leader said, sounding equally impressed and mocking. "You're a powerful little thing, aren't you?"

Mundin scowled up at Mara. "The healer? Tell me you're joking."

"Not that it will get them far," the Hranite snorted before calling up to the top of the ramp. "Because what are you going to do now, little chitling? You're all tired out, and here I am ready for round two. Think you can stop me a second time?"

"Okay, okay," Korent blurted. "We'll tell you. Just promise you'll let us go free."

"I already said you have my word," Mundin said, looking pleased.

"Korent, no!" Ari barked.

Confusion muddled through the exhaustion gripping Mara. They'd already found the stone, so what harm would come from telling the Hranites how it was located? It took her an embarrassingly long time to realize that was exactly the point. Ari and Korent were play-acting to trick Mundin and the Hranites into thinking the stone hadn't been found yet.

"We have to," Korent insisted. "Mara can barely stand up. There's no escape. We can't face that—that *thing* again." He looked down at Mundin. "There's energy in the walls. It creates markers directing which way to go."

Mundin snorted. "Likely."

"Korent, hush," Ari pressed.

"No, it's true. There's one just by the tunnel you came in through. The trail leads that way," Korent pointed toward the opposite tunnel, "deeper into the mountain."

The Hranite leader marched through the mass of her countrymen, shoving aside any that didn't get out of her way fast enough. She examined the tunnel behind them. "He's right. There is energy here."

"Now keep your word and let us go," Korent said.

Mundin looked back at the marked tunnel. "That's the direction we came from." He paused, looking at the tunnel in front of him. "But if this is the way to the stone, then why were you coming back through here?"

"Who says we were?" Korent said quickly. Too quickly.

"Because that tunnel remains straight, and we walked into it with no sign of you, and we returned with no sign of you." Mundin's voice grew stronger with confidence. "You would have had to sneak up behind us and then turn around to go the other way if your claim is true."

"You think it's this way? Further than we went?" the Hranite leader asked, still beside the far tunnel.

"We were confused as to the direction," Ari said, defeat in her voice. "We were just in the process of turning ourselves around when you found us."

Mundin looked at the tunnels again, then at the ramp. "You're lying. Or..." His gaze flickered over the group and stopped on Korent, who gripped his sword with one hand and his pack strap with the other. A slow smile crept across Mundin's face. "Or you already found it."

"No, we didn't," Korent tried, but it was too late.

The Hranite leader ambled closer to the bottom of the ramp, a smug grin widening her skeletal face. "That was slick. But not slick enough."

"And this is much simpler now." Mundin nodded to the leader. "Kill them."

"As you command," the leader said sarcastically. Still, she raised her hands, looking up at them with that same grin.

Ari looked over her shoulder to the corner where Mara slumped. "Mara..."

Mara tried to stand straight and failed. There was no way she could stop another attack. There was nothing any of them could do to fight this. They were dead. She closed her eyes and waited for the sting to come.

Chapter 17

A hissing sound all but vibrated the entire cave. Everyone froze. The hiss grew louder, and then hundreds of underdwellers dropped from the ceiling, pouncing on the Hranites, clawing and dragging at them. Lut landed beside Mara, shrugging his shoulders and making the laughing hiss. Her relief gave her enough strength to throw her arms around him. "Thank you," she whispered.

He cuddled for a moment, then ducked out of her grip, raising both arms high in the air and doing the funny arm-wave dance around Mikell, laugh-hissing all the way.

Mikell scowled, but faced the chaos below. "We have to help them."

"No," Ari countered, helping Mara to her feet and supporting her weight. "We have to get out. They're providing a diversion. We can't ignore the chance to escape."

Mikell bristled. "Run away while others fight in our stead?"

"We have to get the stone out of here and back to the princess," Ari reminded him. "Staying here and fighting them will only keep it within their reach."

"But—" Mikell's scowl deepened, then he shook his head. "Fine. Let's move."

Korent and Mikell led the way down the ramp, using their blades and the underdwellers' diversion to create a clear path to the tunnel. Ari helped Mara along, and Lut scurried at their side, hissing and clawing at any Hranite that got too close.

"Stop them!" the Hranite leader shrieked before three underdwellers jumped on her, knocking her beneath the mass of bodies filling the cave. The Hranites tried to obey, but the underdwellers tripped, bit, and tackled with all the more vigor. The small group rushed along the wall, following the cleared path to the tunnel, and made it through.

Mikell and Korent stopped at the edge of the tunnel long enough for Ari and Mara to get through, then followed behind. A light flicked to life in Ari's hand, and Korent caught it with his torch. The light flashed rapidly as they ran, leaving Mara all the more dizzy.

They kept up their speed, not daring to slow even as the sounds of the fight faded. Lut kept looking back, hissing and baring his teeth. Mara got the impression the fight wasn't going well for his brethren. "Hurry," she strained to say loud enough for the others to hear. "They'll be after us soon."

Mikell scooped her up in his arms, drawing a gasp of surprise, and the group sped up. She closed her eyes, disappointed in herself. She'd been slowing them all down. As usual.

The long tunnel eventually came to a massive hub of tunnels, like spokes on a wheel. Ari pointed to one on the right. "There's a marker here."

"Then we go this way," Korent headed for a tunnel on the opposite side, one that sloped back downwards.

"Down?" Mikell frowned.

"They'll expect us to go upwards, toward the exit, and they know to watch for the energy markers now," Korent explained.

"He's right." Ari followed him. "We have to put more distance between them and us. Then we'll find our way out."

They hurried down the new tunnel. Exhaustion settled deeper over Mara, and the rock walls began to swirl together in the blinking torchlight. She became only faintly aware of the movement and time passing around her before she felt a jarring sensation and realized Mikell was setting her down, speaking to her. She couldn't quite make out the words, but his tone grew more urgent.

Furry fingers pressed a chunk of the slimy moss into her hand. She tried to lift it to her mouth to eat, but her arm wouldn't respond.

More voices danced around her, and she felt the moss at her lips. "Go on, Mara," Ari's no-nonsense tone slipped through the haze. "Take a bite."

She obeyed. As she chewed, her surroundings settled back into order. Mikell cradled her in his arms, clutching her tight. Ari and Korent hovered close and watched in concern. Lut tilted his head at her from where he perched on the ceiling directly above.

Mara finished the bite and took the rest of the moss from Ari. "Thank you." Her voice was still weak, but at least she could speak clearly now.

Ari smiled in relief and nodded. She and Korent sat down, digging waterskins and food out of their packs.

Mikell continued to hold Mara close as she ate the rest of the moss. "I was afraid..."

She pressed a hand against his cheek. "I'm all right, tabe-me. I had never done that before, and it took much of my energy."

"I'm impressed you were able to do that at all," Ari said, leaning back against the rock wall behind her. The cave they rested in was small, a sort of miniature dome at the end of a low tunnel. Apparently the others had deemed it a safe enough place to rest for the moment. "Most healers wouldn't be able to stop a single attack, much less stop three at once."

"I was scared," Mara admitted. "I was afraid I'd be too late." She pushed herself upright, though she still leaned on Mikell. "I'm sorry. I know I slowed us down."

"Raisa-me," Mikell chided as he handed her a waterskin and some food. "You saved us. You have nothing to apologize for."

"Though *you* might," Korent said in a half-teasing tone. He nodded toward Lut on the ceiling. "I believe 'coward' was the term you used?"

Mikell snorted, but finally gave Lut a begrudging nod. "Thanks."

Lut snuffled a couple times and shrugged.

"I wonder how he was able to convince his tribe to defend us," Ari mused. "It wasn't that long ago they attacked us themselves."

"Maybe there's more than one tribe in this mountain," Korent offered.

"But why would so many of them help us?" Mikell eyed Lut again.

"I think I know why," Mara said. "He and I ran into them before. They were hostile at first, but Lut talked to them, and I healed a bunch of them. They were okay with me after that."

"That's a good way to make allies," Ari chuckled.

Mikell gave Mara a tighter squeeze, then asked, "What's the plan now?"

Mara looked back at the low tunnel. "How far off the trail are we?"

"Pretty far," Ari said. "Though I'm not sure we should return to that path. Now that they know what to look for in the walls, they'll be watching that route more closely. It will be better if we find a completely different way through the tunnels."

"How? Do we even know if there's another way out?" Mikell asked.

"There likely is," Korent said. "It's unlikely a system this large would have only one way in or out."

"And how would we go about finding a new exit?" Mikell pressed. "I don't have a map, and I don't believe you have one, either. Those markers were the only way we had any idea of which direction we were going. Are we going to wander these passageways until we all die of exhaustion?"

"We could die of starvation first," Korent supplied in the excessively casual tone he used when joking. "Or freeze. There are plenty of other options."

Mikell scowled.

"What, you have a better idea of how to get out?" Korent raised an eyebrow.

"We get back to the markers. We'll find a way around the Hranites, or fight if we need to."

"We can't risk bringing the stone back in their reach," Ari said, shaking her head. "I understand you prefer being direct, Mikell, but there aren't enough of us to face them. If the underdwellers hadn't shown up when they did, we'd all be dead and the Hranites would have the stone." She glanced up at Lut. "And from the sounds I heard as we fled, I get the feeling we won't be able to count on them for aid again."

Mara kept watching Lut as the others continued their argument. She beckoned him down to her. "Lut, we need to find a way out," she said, pointing in a broad arc. He mimicked the arcing gesture, but didn't seem to understand.

"We need to go outside. We..." She looked around, then dipped her fingers in her waterskin and began drawing on the cave floor. She made a crude ground with a tree and oversized flower, then a sun in the sky. She pointed to it. "There. We need to go there." Lut tilted his head, snarled out a sentence, then wriggled his fingers over the floor as if drawing. He looked at her with a happy shrug. She sighed. He still didn't get it.

She realized that the cave had gone quiet and looked up to see the others watching. "I hoped I could help him understand what we need," she explained, eying the crude drawing in embarrassment. "It was silly."

Ari evaluated the drawing on the floor. "No, I think you have the right idea. Perhaps if we use something more tangible..." She looked around, then took the torch from Korent and stood, raising the light to the highest point of the domed ceiling. "Act like this is the sun." She shielded her eyes from it in overdramatic gestures, blinking and squinting. Mara quickly did the same.

The men stared dumbly. Mara nudged Mikell with her elbow. "It's the sun. That means it's really bright."

"Oh." A look of distaste crinkled his nose, but he and Korent obediently joined in the pantomime.

"See? The sun," Mara said to Lut, making the 'outside' arc again and then repeating the eye-shielding gesture. "The sun."

Lut made his hissing laugh as he watched them all, shrugging repeatedly. He copied their movements.

"He doesn't get it," Mikell said, dropping his arm.

Lut did the gesture again, then stopped. He looked up at the light, shielded himself from it, then looked at Mara and pointed directly upward, beyond the torch. "Yes!" She nodded vigorously and copied his gesture. "Yes, the sun in the sky. Outside. Please, we need to go there."

He did his arm-wave dance around the room, then darted down the tunnel, pausing halfway through to look back at them.

"We can rest longer if we need," Mikell said, looking at Mara.

She could see the lingering concern in his eyes, and she squeezed his hand. "It's best if we move on. The sooner we can get out of here, the better."

Lut led them onward, moving fast enough that they occasionally lost sight of him and had to hurry their pace to catch up. Ari took the torch since she had the easiest time keeping up with him and could provide a clear beacon for the others to follow. Lut paused at a branching of tunnels, snuffling at each one before snarling with joy and scampering onto the wall of one of them that angled downward.

"I hope he really did understand what we want and isn't just leading us further into the mountain," Mikell grunted, frowning at the tunnel before following the underdweller.

"I believe he did," Mara said. "At any rate, this should make it far more difficult for the Hranites to track us. There's no logical reason we would take this route."

"My point exactly," Mikell muttered.

She couldn't help but smile as she took his hand. "It'll be all right, tabe-me. We just have to trust."

They followed Lut through a few more bizarre route choices before finally coming to a tunnel that climbed upward at a moderate slope. Mara had been fighting her own doubts about Lut's understanding, but the worries vanished on seeing the angle. "See? He knows what he's doing."

Lut scampered back to her side, clutching at her leg and hissing franticly. Alarmed, she looked ahead and saw reflections of torchlight off the tunnel walls.

"What's wrong?" Korent looked ahead. "The tunnel's wet. Does he have a problem with water?"

"That isn't water," Mara and Ari said at the same time. Ari glanced at Mara, then stepped forward with curiosity.

"No! Stay away from it." Mara strained her ears for the clicking sound even as she spoke, quiet but urgent. "That's the gel. The stuff the bug monsters use to trap their prey."

Mikell took a step backward. "Then we find a different route. There was another tunnel just a few paces back. We'll take that one instead."

They turned around and entered the new tunnel, but found it blocked only a short distance in by a grayish, bumpy wall. Lut squeaked, reeling backwards and hauling on Mara's arm. Her breath caught in her throat as she realized what she was looking at. The last time she'd seen the monster's segmented shell, it had been toned by a bluish glow. In torchlight, it looked completely different. "Move!" she hissed. "Back, back now!"

"What? What is it?" Mikell demanded.

The terrible clicking noise came, and the 'wall' uncurled itself upward, mandibles snapping at the intruders. Mikell jumped back a step in surprised alarm, yanking his sword out. Lut shrieked and scrambled to retreat, dragging Mara with him. Ari moved steadily backwards, one hand on her waterskin, ready to turn the fluid into a weapon.

Korent stayed by Mikell's side, his own sword ready. "Let's move before it decides we're a threat, brother." Mikell didn't waver, keeping his sword aimed at the monster. "It may not pursue us if we leave quietly," Korent tried again, giving Mikell a firm tug. "Go."

Mara saw the resolution in her husband's stance waver, and she forced herself to slow even as Lut continued pulling at her. "Please, tabe-me," she whispered loud enough for Mikell to hear. "We don't want to fight it. If it might let us go unharmed, we have to try."

Mikell gave her a brief glance, then slowly stepped backwards, his focus on the monster. It clicked its mandibles their way, making Mara and Lut jump, but it still didn't advance on them. Mara forced her breathing to slow. It was going to be okay. They had startled the monster, that was all. She centered her focus on the monster's numerous eyes. *These aren't a threat. Back to sleep. Not a threat. Back to sleep.*

The monster reared back and unleashed a spray of gel. A spray of water from Ari intercepted most of the goo, with only splatters landing on Mikell and Korent. Mikell shouted and charged. The monster lashed with its mandibles, knocking him sideways.

Korent and Ari crossed each other, him tossing her a waterskin and her waving the torch and shouting for the monster's attention, creating an opening for Korent to dart in and strike. The monster let out that terrible grinding noise of pain, its legs flailing at Korent. To Mara's shock and horror, one of the legs pierced Korent's side. Tiny daggers of ice shot across the space into the leg and closest carapace, making the grinding noise louder. Korent was able to stagger out of the monster's reach while it was occupied by Ari's attack. He stumbled backwards, blood from the wound looking like oil staining his side in the torchlight.

Lut almost pulled Mara off her feet in his frantic attempt at fleeing with her in tow. "No, I can't leave my friends!" She twisted her arm free. Korent was close enough now that she could reach his shoulder, and she sent healing energy through his body to the source of the wound. Lut hissed and darted up the wall.

Mikell regained his feet and lunged again, aiming for the monster's underbelly. It recovered in time to intercept his sword with its powerful mandibles, the sword catching fast in its grip. Mikell kicked at it and ducked, managing to shift his sword free and roll away before the thing could snap at him again.

Lut jumped off the ceiling and landed on the monster's head, clinging to the shell with his feet while digging and clawing at its eyes. The grinding noise all but shook the tunnel as the monster thrashed. Mikell took advantage of the moment and darted in for a strike, slicing through the thinner shell on its underside. Fluid spurted out, yellowish in the torchlight, and splattered across

Mikell's arm and face. He stumbled and fell backwards with a cry of pain like a dagger to Mara's heart. She lunged toward him, but Ari caught her arm before she could get in range of the monster's wild flailing.

"Korent!" Ari barked. She flung another barrage of ice daggers, forcing the monster to rear and stumble back. Korent darted in, grabbed Mikell, and dragged his friend clear.

Lut snarled and smashed both fists into the monster's eyes. The grinding noise turned into a terrible, high-pitched whine that pierced Mara's ears like someone was trying to drive a sharpened stick through them into her brain. The monster slammed upwards, smashing Lut into the top of the tunnel, then dropped back down. Lut fell from his perch and rolled limply across the tunnel floor.

Ari tossed her waterskin in the air, and it exploded in a burst of ice shards driving into the monster. As it reeled from the attack, Ari grabbed Lut. "Go!"

Korent half-dragged Mikell out of the tunnel into the darkness, Mara following closely behind. Ari emerged just after, carrying Lut over one shoulder and holding the torch high in the other hand. They ran back the way they'd come until they could no longer hear the grinding and whining sounds behind them.

Korent stumbled and dropped into an alcove. "Here. We can rest here."

Mara knelt by Mikell. "Hold the light steady." As Korent took the torch from Ari, Mara sucked in a breath. The splattered drops hissed and sizzled on her husband's skin, turning the light brown flesh a vile shade of green. He rasped against the pain, fighting to stay awake.

Ari dug into her pack after she set Lut beside Mikell. "I'll clean it off him. You see to their wounds."

Mara nodded, grasping Mikell and Lut's hands and releasing her healing energy to do its work. It wasn't clear how much time passed before Mikell stopped shaking and Lut made a few snubbling grunts, pushing himself up in disorientation, but Ari had already finished cleaning the rest of the monster's toxic blood from Mikell's skin.

The Kadrian rested next to Korent, sharing a small portion of their remaining food. She pushed more toward the three of them. "Eat. We need to keep moving as soon as everyone's ready."

Lut squeezed Mara tight, snarling in a scolding manner. He then sniffed at the dried meat, recoiled in distaste, and vanished down the tunnel.

"I guess meat isn't part of their diet," Mara said, handing the piece back to Ari.

Ari nodded and passed around a waterskin. "Only drink a little. I'm afraid I had to use up more of our water than I'd intended."

Mikell munched on his food quietly, occasionally rubbing at his arm where the blood had burned him. He was clearly shaken. Mara curled closer to him, offering what comfort she could. Lut returned and plopped on her other side, happily chowing away at something Mara couldn't identify.

When Mikell finally spoke, it was directed past Mara toward Lut. "Thank you for helping us. We may not have gotten away if you hadn't attacked it as you did."

Lut tilted his head, staring blankly.

Mikell paused, then gave a careful, deliberate bow.

The underdweller made his laughing hiss, mimicked the bow, then jumped into his arm-wave dance. Mara, Korent, and Ari laughed, and even Mikell managed to smile.

By the time they'd finished eating and had something to drink, Mikell seemed to have recovered his composure. "We best go quickly. We don't know how far away the Hranites are at this point."

"We'll need a different way around." Mara shuddered at the thought of running into any more of the monsters. "Somewhere that avoids that nest."

Lut already sniffed around at the tunnel, crawling up the walls to crane his neck and draw in long huffs of the dank cave air. He snarled excitedly and took off.

"I guess we've found our new route," Korent said, helping Ari to her feet and hurrying after their underdweller guide.

Lut led them through another maze of tunnels, sometimes up, sometimes down, sometimes seeming to go in circles. As the hours dragged on, Mara found it harder and harder to maintain their rapid pace.

The others were slowing, too, and eventually Lut was forced to come back and move at a steady crawl along the ceiling rather than at his normal scamper. They occasionally heard sounds of movement, and Lut was quick to lead them in the opposite direction, though his snarls turned more concerned and tense each time they heard it.

Mara stumbled over some loose rocks and recovered her balance before Mikell steadied her. She wanted to curl up and sleep for days, but that wasn't an option. She wouldn't ask for a break, either; she wasn't about to slow everyone down again. That, and her own eagerness to get out of the oppressive caves and back into sunlight and fresh air, kept her feet marching onward. She realized that the ground felt softer beneath her feet. The solid rock had shifted to rocky soil. Hope fluttered inside her. Were they finally almost out?

"Look at that." Korent's tone was quiet, but not so quiet that they couldn't hear the lilt of excitement as he lowered the torch for a better look at the ground. "We have to be close."

Lut hissed a couple times and picked up speed again. Mara's body complained fervently, but she pressed on, forcing herself to move faster and keep up. She felt just as excited as Korent.

Their underdweller guide slowed as the tunnel opened up into a larger space, more long than wide. He sniffed, hissing, then hugged the wall around the side of the room, scooting forward more slowly now.

Mikell put out a protective hand in front of Mara, his body tense as he eyed the room. "What is it?" he whispered. "Does he sense something?"

Mara remembered how Lut had acted when the other underdwellers had found them, how tense he had gotten. She saw the same tightness in Lut's body now. "I think so." She kept her voice as low as possible. "Stay quiet."

The other two seemed to pick up on the sense of caution and moved carefully behind Lut, watching for loose rocks or other things which might give away their passage through the space. Mara looked around as she crept along the wall, trying to see where the threat might come from. The light didn't reach much, but she could make out the form of two other tunnels near the one they'd come from, and one tunnel leaving the room ahead of them.

They approached an opening in the wall beside them, but Lut didn't seem concerned about it, sliding past with hardly a glance, so that wasn't the threat. Mara took a peek as she followed. The narrow opening led to what appeared to be an enclosed alcove, nothing more.

Lut's hissing intensified sharply enough to alarm the hairs on the back of Mara's neck. She froze, as did the others, seeking out what had frightened Lut.

She didn't have to look long. Figures emerged from the tunnel ahead of them, sidling into the dim reach of the torchlight. Hranites.

She spun and saw more figures spilling out from one of the other tunnels behind them, cutting off their retreat. It took her brain a moment to process the squatty underdwellers at the lead of each group, their hands tied over their heads, ropes forming crude leashes around their necks. The fight hadn't gone well for the underdwellers, and the Hranites had apparently forced their prisoners to lead them to the most likely exit. They must have prepared this trap while she and her friends took longer to work their way here.

Mikell already had his sword drawn, his form braced in a defensive stance, his other arm pushing Mara further behind him. Lut clung to her leg. On her other side, Korent braced in a similar fashion in front of Ari, who had a waterskin in hand and ready. Mara looked around, desperate to find some other exit, some escape route she'd missed in her previous examination. But the only exit near them was the alcove they had just passed, and she doubted there was any further escape from there. They'd only be trapped in a smaller space.

"Do you think the underdwellers will help again?" Korent whispered.

"No." Mara tried to keep her voice from shaking. "I don't think so. They were already beaten once, and I don't think they would attack and risk their friends being killed." She felt sick to her stomach, remembering all too well what it was like to be helpless and threatened so enemies could control her friends. She pressed herself further against the wall. She wouldn't let that happen again, not ever.

"So glad you finally made it," Mundin said, standing at the front of the group that had come up behind them. His sneering voice sent another splash of nausea through Mara's system. "I'm afraid you won't find any allies to help you escape this time. Now," he gestured to the Hranite leader standing at his side, "shall we pick up where we left off?"

Ari eyed him, her face hard. But her attention shifted to the Hranites. "I suppose he's told you everything you need to know about the stone."

"Not until we have it," the Hranite leader hissed. She grinned. "Better motivation for us to get our hands on it quickly."

"Then he hasn't told you about the danger it presents."

Mara watched closely for their reactions. Did they know about the entity possessing the stone?

The leader laughed along with many of her compatriots. "Yes, how it presents a danger to the person wielding it. That's why he will wield it first so we know how to control the threat."

Ari's face relaxed, and her lips crept into the tiniest smile. "Oh. Is that all he's told you?"

"Until we have secured it, yes." The leader hissed impatiently. "You are stalling."

"Hardly. I was merely curious if he had bothered to tell you that the stone uses its wielder to try to kill everyone else nearby."

The Hranites shifted in displeasure, suspicious rumblings passing between them. Several took a half-step closer to Mundin, and the leader's vertical eyes narrowed at him.

"I don't know what she's talking about," Mundin snapped, his tone holding a sharp edge. "Either she's making it up, or it's something that was never mentioned in the journals."

"I'm also curious as to whose idea it was that Mundin should test the stone first," Ari continued in an overly casual voice.

All the Hranites' eyes fixed on Mundin. The leader's eyes slitted further.

"She's trying to turn us against each other," Mundin blurted. "Don't let her trick you."

"I just find it very hard to believe that the royals who wrote those journals, who made sure to note that the stone presents a danger to its user, would fail to mention the equal danger to anyone near the user," Ari said. "It seems out of character to me. So either they 'conveniently' forgot to mention crucial information..." She eyed Mundin. "Or he did."

"She's lying!" Mundin shouted, his face red. "She—"

Whatever else he was going to say came out in a gurgle as a sword tip broke through his chest.

Mara gasped and looked away, feeling ill once more. He was a despicable man, but she still couldn't handle watching such brutality. A thump signaled that it was over.

The leader wiped her blade off on his back, then stepped over his body and faced them. "This is simpler, then. Give us the stone."

"You already heard it's too dangerous to be used," Ari said.

"I heard your claims. I'm sure we'll still find a use for it. Now give it…" The leader stopped, then smiled. "Pardon me. I'm being quite foolish. There's no need for you to give it to us when we can simply take it." She lifted her hands.

Mikell cried out in alarm and pain, Ari and Korent doing the same. Mara clutched her husband and saw the bulge moving up his arm. She focused on creating a wall even as her mind raced. Why had she been spared? The wall fell into place, the bulge vanished, and Mikell dropped forward, bent double and gasping.

At that instant, Mara felt the sting in her hand, followed by the shredding pain as the bulge tore its way up her arm, drawing screams from her throat. She walled it off before it could get any higher, her mind already forming connections and creating a new plan.

She shoved Mikell and Lut into the alcove, then grabbed Ari and Korent, yanking them in after her and shoving them to the sides. "Get out of her line of sight! She has to see you to hurt you!" She pressed her back tightly against the wall and prayed she was right. Sure enough, once the others were out of sight of the tunnel outside, they gasped in relief as the bulges vanished.

"Clever, little chitling," the Hranite's voice came from outside. "Clever indeed. And now what? Is there an exit in there you'll crawl out through?"

Mara looked around the small space, but she already knew there wasn't.

"So you and your friends are trapped there," the leader continued. "How long do you think you'll last, the four of you—excuse me, three fighters and one useless little healer—against all of us, even with a bit of cover to help you?"

"Hardly useless, after she beat you," Mikell retorted.

"Beat me? You mean stopped me." Mara could hear the smirk in the leader's voice. "Temporarily." She said something to the others behind her, and thundering feet charged forward.

Mikell pushed Mara back away from the opening, taking her place with his sword ready.

"Stay out of her sight!" Mara reminded him and Korent. Both of them stopped just short of the opening, staying close to the wall and lashing out at the Hranites that tried to enter.

Ari flung ice shards from one waterskin, then drew the water from the other one into a sphere that solidified and blasted its way out of the alcove, bashing into kneecaps as it went. "What's the plan?" she asked loudly enough for the others to hear her over the din of crashing blades and shouts of pain from outside their shelter.

"Keep taking them down as fast as they can come," Korent puffed, blocking an incoming strike and returning one of his own.

Lut danced from side to side, agitated and hissing in distress. Mara looked up at the ceiling. The entrance to the alcove stretched from the floor to the ceiling, relatively high above their heads. "If you go, they might not see you," she said. "You might even be able to help your captured friends." He wouldn't be able to understand what she said, she knew, and she crouched beside him, looking into his anxious eyes. "Go," she said, pointing to the opening at the ceiling and nodding. "It's okay."

He hissed, looked at the opening, then at her, and back again. Then he snarled and scooted himself flat against the wall beside Mikell, grabbing and yanking at any ankles that came within his reach. Mikell and Korent fluidly adjusted to the new tactical advantage, letting Lut create another layer of chaos while they fought those that remained unaffected by Lut's tripping grasp or Ari's water sphere.

Mikell's swings were getting sloppier. Mara put a hand on his shoulder and gave him a fresh burst of energy, but not too much. It was hard to say how much healing would be needed through this fight. Korent and Ari looked just as worn out. Mara could hardly recall how long it had been since they'd all truly rested. The Hranite leader's words echoed through her mind. How long could they last against the ceaseless attackers?

Korent grunted as a strike got through his defense, drawing a heavy red line across his arm. Mara reached for him and felt an immediate sting in her hand. She quickly withdrew before the leader could continue the attack. They were genuinely trapped, and she couldn't even help half the people standing in her defense. She focused on sending healing energy across the distance, controlling it tightly so it was only enough to close the wound and numb the pain. She wouldn't be able to do even that before too much longer.

Ari dug into her pack, then tossed it aside and grabbed at Korent's. "I need more water!"

Mikell made an abrupt slash forward, forcing several attackers back, and Korent took the moment to shrug the pack off. Ari pulled it back with her as Korent resumed fighting. She dug through and came up with one partially-filled waterskin.

She looked over at Mara, her eyes voicing her thoughts: she, like Mara, realized how trapped they were, how unlikely they were to get out alive. All the more so once they ran out of water for Ari to use as her weapon—and it looked like that wouldn't be long. The Kadrian's trembling hand slipped once more into the bag and withdrew a cloth-covered mass.

Mara wasn't able to hold back the gasp, and she pressed her hands over her mouth. She hadn't gotten much more than a vague sense of the shadowy entity that had possessed Ari, and that faint understanding was enough to make her whole body quake.

Korent saw the alarm in Mara's eyes, glanced over his shoulder, and realized what Ari held. "No. Don't you dare."

"It only got to me when I tried to do something I couldn't do before," Ari said, though her expression indicated she'd rather take Korent's order than hold the mass in her hands a moment longer. "If I stick with things I'm accustomed to doing, it should be all right."

Mikell dropped to one knee with a gasp of pain, a jagged blade grinding into his shoulder. Korent managed to knock the blade away, and Mara pressed a hand on her husband's back, closing the wound as fast as possible.

"It isn't a choice." Ari sounded like she was trying to convince herself rather than the others. "We can't let them get this. We can't risk losing this fight."

"Ari—" Korent struggled to hold his defense against a thick-muscled Hranite that swung with pounding blow after pounding blow.

Determination overtook the fear in Ari's eyes. She dug through the cloth, pulled the stone free, and focused on it.

A faint roar grew louder as air rushed in from the tunnel leading out of the mountain. Shouts of surprise and alarm followed shortly as the gust of wind increased in power. The closest attackers took a pace back, trying to assess the new threat.

"No you don't," the leader snarled from outside the alcove.

Ari jerked, her eyes wide in sudden agony, too frozen by the pain to even scream. A choking sound came from her throat. The bulge climbing her arm was twice as large as the ones before, large enough to be seen through her long sleeves, and moving even faster.

"Ari!" Korent cried, dividing his attention between the paused fight and the Kadrian. Lut scampered up the wall to the ceiling, chittering in alarm.

Panic shot through Mara like an arrow. She lunged across the alcove, aiming a hand at Ari's shoulder and focusing on the wall. The speeding bulge was nearly at the place she aimed. She closed her eyes and focused harder, as if she could supplement her willpower to drive the wall into place.

Her energy formed the wall, and the bulge vanished. Ari crumpled. Korent instinctively caught her with his free arm before she hit the floor, and the stone tumbled loose from her grip, rolling freely toward the Hranites.

"Mikell!" Mara shouted, scrambling after the stone herself.

He lunged for it, but his reaction was a fraction too slow. Mara brushed past him in pursuit, hardly noticing the startled Hranites around her that were no longer distracted by the now-dissipated wind blast. The leader snarled in challenge as the stone rolled toward her, and she moved to intercept. Mara leapt in desperation, throwing her whole body after it, and the leader did the same. Their hands clamped around the stone at the exact same moment.

Chapter 18

Mikell

No one moved, staring in shocked silence at the two women. Mara lay on her belly on the floor, her arms outstretched, hands clamped around the stone. The Hranite leader was in the exact same position on the other side. Their eyes were fixed on each other, unblinking, and they were unnaturally still. Almost like Ari had looked when the stone took her over.

"Stop! Get away from that thing!" Mikell lunged forward to tear his wife away from the dangerous stone.

The Hranites had been caught off-guard by the sudden appearance of a tiny woman darting around them, but a warrior was something they understood. They slashed at him, forcing him back. He swung franticly, blocking and trying to drive them back and form an opening to reach his wife. Another Hranite smirked and stood over Mara, raising his sword.

"No!" Mikell howled, slashing all the more desperately.

The Hranite swung. Before his blade reached the petite Elf woman, a flash of light burst from the stone. The Hranite, along with his weapon, went flying.

Even those attacking Mikell stopped at that, and the Hranites shifted further away from the stone, leaving a generous circle around the two women.

Mikell cautiously moved forward, watching to see if the Hranites would attack him again, but they were all focused on Mara and the leader. He looked at his wife, at her stoic, still face. It was like she was locked in some sort of battle of wills against the Hranite leader. There had to be something he could do to help.

"Mikell, stop!" Korent said. He knelt on the ground, supporting a dazed Ari. "There's nothing you can do to help. You'll only get yourself hurt."

"I can't..." Mikell stared at the silent combatants. He couldn't just stand back and leave his wife to fight unaided. And yet he knew Korent was right; there was nothing he could do.

No one moved for a long time, watching, waiting to see what would happen. Then Mara let out a little gasp. She blinked and looked at the leader with something that was almost like pity.

The leader's eyes went wide just as another flash of light came from the stone. The Hranite woman went flying across the space, slammed into the rock wall, and fell into a heap on the ground.

Mara carefully stood, hugging the stone to her chest.

"Raisa-me, come here," Mikell barked, hardly able to speak through his relief. His wife was okay. Now he had to keep her that way.

But the Hranites cautiously stepped closer to her, thickening the circle and blocking her route to Mikell. His instinct was to attack, but with so many so close to her—he couldn't risk attacking and motivating them to strike at her.

One of the Hranites eyed her. "You will do to us like she did to you," he said, his gravelly voice halting as if he didn't often speak their language.

Mara shuddered, her head reflexively shaking no and clutching the stone closer.

The speaker laughed, then said something in the Hranite language. The others grinned and moved closer, their weapons raised.

"No! Mara!" Mikell lunged, but his blade only met metal, several Hranites turning to face him as the rest swarmed Mara. He could barely see her anymore, only brief flashes between movements around her. "Mara!"

Her luminescent eyes flicked his direction, then focused on the stone. Her mouth moved around a word he couldn't hear through the chaos.

The Hranites stumbled as if they were suddenly worn out. Their weapons clumped and clattered against the floor, the handles barely gripped in weak hands.

In the perplexed silence, he could hear her next word. "Calm."

The Hranites blinked, looking all the more confused now.

"Okay," Mikell said quickly. "Now put the stone down."

"Sleep," Mara whispered.

The Hranites slumped to the floor and didn't move again.

Mikell hurried to work his way toward her, stumbling and jumping over the collapsed enemy. "Good, good job. Now put the stone down. Do you hear me? You have to—"

The invisible dagger hit him in the chest, just like it had when Ari used the stone. He staggered, gasping. "Raisa-me, drop the stone. You have to let it go!"

He had no way to tell if she'd heard him. Her eyes remained fixed on the stone. The previous battle of wills had been against an arrogant Hranite; this battle was against an evil entity that had far more practice at this style of combat.

"Mara, listen to us!" Korent called, pain in his voice.

Ari had said she didn't realize it was truly happening until she heard Korent calling her. "Mara, you have to fight it," Mikell pressed, struggling to move closer to her against the pain driving deeper into his chest by the moment. "You have to break free. Mara!"

No change. He wanted to reach for her and tear the stone from her hands, but he knew the stone would only blast him across the room.

"Mara!" Korent echoed, louder this time. "You have to hear us!"

Dark shadows pooled into Mara's eyes. The dagger ground in deep enough that Mikell could hardly breathe. "Mara!" His voice seemed weak. His legs wanted to give out on him. There was no color left in his wife's eyes now, only the swirling shadows.

He wouldn't let it take her. He gritted his teeth, his eyes now fixed on the stone. It would attack him, no question, but if he could grab it fast enough and hold on, then the force would tear the stone free from her hands. She couldn't hear them, and he didn't have enough breath left in his lungs to speak even if she could. This was the only way.

He focused all his strength and willpower into the task before him. His legs wouldn't hold him up much longer. If he was to have a chance, it had to be now. He clenched his fists, staggered a pace closer, then lunged and clamped both hands around the stone, driving every ounce of strength and will into his grip.

It was like he'd been trapped inside a bolt of lightning, the power crackling through his body from one arm to the other, smashing at anything it could reach along the way—muscle, lungs, heart. The world shifted around him. A hand clamped on his shoulder, and everything swirled into green.

He first realized he no longer hurt. That was a pleasant change. He second realized that he was no longer holding the stone, instead standing alone with no one else in sight. His final realization was that he no longer stood in the cave room but on a swirling green haze. No walls around him or ceiling above him, just more of the haze. It was like he was somehow suspended inside a cloud. A green cloud.

He turned slowly, testing his footing and finding it curiously solid in spite of there being nothing solid to stand on. A break in the sea of green caught his attention. Mara lay on her side a couple paces from him, her eyes fixed open and glassy.

His breath caught, and he rushed to her side. "Mara!" He gripped her shoulders. She couldn't be dead. He wouldn't allow it. "MARA!"

She blinked and gasped as if he'd shaken her from a deep dream. She stared at him. "Tabe-me?"

All he could do was pull her tight to him, wanting to weep with relief. He kissed her hair, then drew back to examine her. "Are you hurt?"

She seemed confused, looking over him, then herself. "I... I don't think so."

He pulled her to her feet and hugged her tight again. Now that the immediate concern was alleviated, he returned his attention to their surroundings. "Where are we?"

"Inside the stone," Ari said from behind him.

He turned, startled, and found her standing there, examining the haze as if she could find some hidden meaning. "What?"

She glanced at him briefly before resuming her visual hunt. "I saw you entering. It was only by Maker's favor I reached you in time to join you."

So many questions—the first of which being, are you insane?—shot forward that they jumbled at his mouth and nothing came out for a moment. He shook his head, forcing the chaos back. "Inside the stone? What are you talking about? We can't be inside the stone."

"And yet here we are."

Her calmness in moments of confusion always aggravated him, but never so much as now. "That's insane. The stone is—" He gestured with his hands, indicating the rough size of the stone.

"Of course we're not physically inside it. Our energies are, though. And since our energies are, essentially, us..." She shrugged.

"Energies? Like magic?" Mara asked. She looked around. "But we look like us."

"Remember how you saw the rocks seem to light up, and I said your mind was interpreting what your energy sensed as something it could see?"

"Oh." Mara looked around again.

"But I don't use magic," Mikell scowled. "You have to be mistaken."

Ari hesitated, her hunt disrupted briefly by a new hunt for the right wording. "That could be less true than you think."

His eyes narrowed. "What are you talking about?"

She sighed. "There's no easy way to say this." She shrugged again, then gave a wry smile. "Congratulations, Mikell. You're a magic user."

He stared, too stunned to speak, the sheer ridiculousness of her statement all but overwhelming him.

Mara stared at Ari, then at him, then back to Ari. "What?"

"You're insane," were the first words to make it through the shock holding Mikell mute. "I don't use magic."

Ari shrugged. "Use magic, no, but you have enough of the magic energy inside of you that you could. It's not much, which is why it's gone unnoticed until now. But your desperation to rescue your wife brought it out by instinct."

"You're insane!" Mikell burst out again, louder this time. "I'm not a magic user."

Ari waved a hand around, swirling the green haze as she repeated herself. "And yet here we are."

Mikell sputtered. This was crazy. He was no magic user. "I'm not... You can't possibly think... there's no way!"

Ari was no longer looking at him, looking past him instead. "I believe we have larger problems at hand."

He turned. At first all he saw was the same swirling green haze, but then he spotted it. Tiny dots of black seemed to appear from the swirls, cast off by the rolling movements. The dots coalesced together, spiraling through the haze to combine into blobs, and those combined into small masses, all coming together into one larger whole.

Mikell started to reach for his sword, but remembered that they were nothing but energy inside of a stone. Of course he didn't have a sword. He placed himself between Mara and the forming entity all the same, unsure how well he could combat it without a weapon but certain that he would do whatever it took to keep the thing away from his wife.

The green haze behind the shadows shrank and vanished as the masses joined, creating a dark form that towered above them. The shadows churned like the green haze, but faster, almost angrily. Some spots were lighter, others darker. It seemed to draw light into itself, making even the air around it grow dim. The only light areas were two violent blue spots high on the entity's surface, flashing like bolts of lightning. The two spots seemed to fix on them like eyes.

"Move," Ari abruptly commanded, darting to the right. Mikell instinctively went left, pulling Mara with him. A wide column of black shadow struck the place they'd been moments before, sending the green haze into mad swirls around the sudden movement.

Ari braced herself a few paces away, extending a hand toward the entity. Mikell saw nothing, but the haze formed an agitated line shooting from her hand to the entity, marking the path of her attack. The entity reeled back. It made no sound, but the air around them vibrated low and painful, as if with a silent roar.

"Raisa-me," he started, ready to command her to run the opposite direction as far as the haze would reach, but she moved further to the left, stepping out from behind him and extending her hand. Another agitated line shot to the entity. It shook, and more columns lashed out, moving like whips to snap at the two women. Ari dodged, and Mara ducked and skittered to one side, avoiding the attack.

Mikell tried to grab the nearest limb-like column, but his hands sank through as if nothing was there. It snapped backwards, then smashed into him, now solid enough to send him tumbling across the formless floor. He scrambled back to his feet, wincing at the ache in his chest where the entity had struck.

"Use your sword!" Ari shouted at him.

"I don't have it!" He lunged forward, trying to grab one of the limbs again. She of all people should know the foolishness of her directions. She was the one who told them they were nothing but energy.

"You do! Draw it and strike," she insisted.

Another limb caught him across the side, but this time he was able to roll with the momentum and regain his feet a few paces away. "No, I don't! We're just energy in here." He spread his hands briefly to fully display his sides, sword and scabbard absent.

Ari shot off another blast at the entity, then charged at Mikell. "Mikell, you spineless, honorless coward!" she screamed, then slapped him across the face.

Rage turned his vision red, and his sword was in hand before he knew what he was doing. "How dare you—" He stopped with realization, staring dumbly at his weapon. How could it have materialized out of nothing?

Ari grabbed his shoulders and aimed him toward the entity. "Good. Now hit it!" She darted back to the side, firing off another blast as she went, dodging and weaving around the limbs smashing in her direction.

One of those limbs landed close to Mikell, and he slashed at it. The blade shot through the limb, severing a mass of dark shadow, and the entity roiled backwards, sending the air into mad vibrations once more.

Mara sent a shot at the eyelights above, and it struck her, knocking her back several paces.

"Mara!" Mikell shouted, lunging toward her, but more limbs flew at him, forcing his attention on his own defense. When he could spare another glance, Mara had already regained her feet and was firing off another strike.

Ari fired for the eyelights as well. "This isn't doing enough," she shouted to them. "We need to find a way to bring it down!"

Mikell lobbed off the end of another limb. Normally he would aim for head, throat, chest, and abdomen to end an enemy, but this was just a shadow. There was only one thing that might be a sensitive area—the eyelights—and the women were already attacking those. "Keep going for the eyes," he called. "I can't reach them myself."

"No, that's not it," Ari grunted out as she dodged another limb smashing her direction. She fired lower this time, then another spot. "Mikell, keep the limbs busy. Mara, strike whatever you can."

Mara weaved around two limbs coming at her and fired one blast after another at the entity, striking random points. Mikell fought his way closer to the shadow itself, slashing at limbs until the entity was forced to turn its focus on driving him back. One of the limbs caught him square in the chest, knocking the air from his lungs and sending him tumbling.

He struggled back to his feet and charged again, taking off half of a limb striking at Mara before driving his way closer. He'd nearly reached the shadow form itself when the entity shot backwards, reeling and shaking the air hard enough that Mikell had to press his hands over his ears.

"That's it!" Ari shot again, and the haze swirls traced a line from her hand to a spot toward the center of the mass, the darkest spot visible. "Aim for that!"

Mara blasted the target, and the entity reeled back further. Encouraged, Mikell charged, swinging madly at any limb he could reach. The spot in question was too high for him to reach with his sword, but he could keep it occupied while the women continued their attack.

Myriad limbs shot out from the entity at the same time, too many to counter. He slashed and fought, but finally a couple of them caught him, wrapping around him and then hurling him away. He staggered back to his feet, sword miraculously still in hand. Mara shrieked as she tried to duck under one of the limbs attacking her, but another three wrapped around her, lifting her off her feet and squeezing tightly.

"Mara!" Mikell scrambled to get back to the fight, but even more limbs flailed at him now.

Ari dodged and weaved, managing to duck under and even jump over several of the limbs reaching for her. Finally there were too many for her to dodge, and she was caught. The limbs wrapped tightly around her, too, lifting her opposite Mara.

"Keep striking," Ari strained out, squirming until she had a hand free to send off another blast at the weak spot. The entity roared, but seemed more like it was angry rather than hurt.

Mikell lobbed off another limb and found three more replacing it.

Mara struggled, but couldn't get her arm through the mass holding her captive.

"It's not enough!" Mikell shouted. He tried to work his way toward Mara to free her. Five limbs flew at him simultaneously. He managed to cut two and dodge one, but the others slammed into him, sending him tumbling once more.

"At the same time," Ari wheezed.

"I can't get free!" Mara's voice was weak from the grip crushing her.

Ari pressed a hand against the limb around her, and it jerked at her attack, but didn't release her. She grunted in frustration and aimed toward Mara. Energy displaced the swirls into madness between them and struck one of the limbs gripping the petite Elf. Again, the limb jerked and writhed without releasing. However, Mara was able to squirm a hand free through the movement.

Mikell saw more limbs headed for them as he regained his feet. He charged, swinging and shouting to force the entity to redirect its attack. Both women fired on the dark spot at the same time. The air shook and the monster flailed, but still it lashed out, catching Mikell once more with an overwhelming attack.

"It didn't—" Mara's sentence cut off in a choking sound.

"Mikell," Ari strained out. "You have to hit it, too!"

Mikell coughed, sucking in ragged breaths and feeling the pain of the repeated battering through his whole body. "I can't get high enough to reach that!"

Ari shook her head. "Throw your sword! Now!" She fired a fresh blast at the spot. Mara did the same.

Mikell dodged another strike from the entity, then shifted his weight backward and hurled his sword. The two women's energy attacks hit the dark spot just moments before his blade hit and sank in, even the hilt disappearing into the darkness. The entity's cry was audible this time, a terrible scream that shook the space hard enough to knock Mikell from his feet.

The limbs flailed and writhed, leaving Ari and Mara tumbling to the floor beneath the madly lashing creature. Mikell caught them both and yanked them to him, sheltering them from the chaos, all three of them covering their ears lest they burst from the powerful sounds and vibrations tearing through the space around them.

The entity seemed to fold in on itself, shrinking the whole mass tighter and tighter. Limbs flew at them but could no longer reach to attack. It continued to roil, as if struggling to flee from whatever force sucked in inward, but soon there was nothing left but a tiny sphere of darkness. Even that quickly tightened until it blinked from existence, and the agitated haze gradually settled down into the normal, peaceful swirls.

Mikell loosened his grip on the women, sitting back and taking slow breaths to recover his composure. He felt as if he'd been running for a day and a half without stop. Ari and Mara seemed likewise exhausted.

He stared at the serene green haze where the entity had vanished, his mind struggling to make sense of what had just happened. The entity itself was easy enough to understand. It was an enemy, they found its weak spot, they defeated it. But the part where he'd had no sword and suddenly had a sword was beyond his grasp. He realized it was also perplexing that he'd managed to grab both women simultaneously; they'd been far out of his reach and in opposite directions.

"Everyone in one piece?" Ari finally asked.

"More or less, I think." Mara's voice was steadier now.

"I didn't have a sword." Mikell patted his sides again, half-expecting another sword to miraculously appear, but of course nothing was there. "And how did I reach the two of you? It's not possible."

Ari eyed him. "Like I said before. Your mind was interpreting what it didn't understand, just like how Mara saw the rocks seem to light up." She paused. "Come to think of it, you said that you saw torchlight reflect off the stone for a moment, but there was nothing reflective in that rock. And the way you kept noticing the imbued rocks... I should have realized then that you had more energy in you than we'd previously known."

Mikell scowled, disliking the direction of conversation. "What's that have anything to do with swords appearing from nowhere?"

"Mara and I are used to extending our energy beyond ourselves, so it was simple for us to use it to attack the creature. You needed something that would feel more tangible. The sword was your mind's way of understanding how to use your energy as a weapon."

Mara's eyes warmed with understanding. "So when he threw his sword, that was actually him attacking with his energy."

"Exactly."

Mikell's scowl deepened, but he had no rational explanation to counter anything Ari had said. "And grabbing the two of you from so far away?"

"Energy has no physical limits of reach." Ari shrugged. "Your protective instincts took over and allowed you to reach us, even when your mind would have said such a thing is impossible. Thank you for that, by the way. I doubt I'd had the presence of mind to get myself to a safe distance at that point."

Mara cuddled closer to Mikell. "You kept us safe. Thank you."

He held her tight, still not sure how to feel about it all.

Ari cleared her throat, looking awkward. "And I need to say... that is, I must apologize for hitting you. And for calling you those things. I hoped your anger would get you to respond instinctively."

Mikell again eyed the spot where the entity had once been. "It worked."

"Still, it wasn't very nice of me."

He shook his head. "You did what you had to. We might not have beaten it if you hadn't. I'm just surprised your ancestors didn't get rid of that thing before they hid it."

"Tashan's ancestors," Ari said with a faintly indifferent tone, as if her mind were elsewhere. "It's entirely possible they didn't know how to defeat it. I certainly wouldn't have known how to enter here. I didn't even know such a thing was possible."

"But I didn't either," Mikell said. "I was just trying to get it away from Mara."

"And you were focused on that task, yes? Intensely focused?"

"Yes, but..." He broke off. Mara spoke often about how much focus was required for magic use.

He pushed the thoughts aside; he had accepted that Mara used magic, but he wasn't interested in thinking about anything beyond that. Taking a look around, he said, "I'm more concerned about what we do now. How do we get out?" He and Mara both looked at Ari, waiting for her instructions.

Ari shrugged. "I have no idea."

Mikell stared. "We're stuck here?"

"Not necessarily. We just don't know how to get out."

"That's the same thing."

"Stuck implies there is no way out." Ari stood and brushed herself off, taking a slow look around. "Not knowing implies there could be a way, and we just haven't found it yet."

"What should we look for?" Mara asked, also standing. Mikell joined her, though he was unable to find the same optimism his wife apparently had.

"Any idea how far we've moved from where we initially entered?" Ari asked.

Mikell looked at the sea of green haze surrounding them. "How would we even tell?"

They all looked around a moment longer. "I guess we just have to pick a direction and start walking," Ari finally said.

"Should we split up?" Mara asked.

Mikell's grip on his wife's hand tightened instinctively. "No."

"He's right," Ari agreed. "We don't know enough about this place to know if it's safe to split up. Best to stay close."

"So which way?" Mikell asked.

Ari shrugged. "Pick one."

Mikell turned around a few times before finally choosing a direction. He walked forward as if confident he'd found the right way, but in reality, there was no difference between this and any other direction. For all he knew, they'd be wandering through green haze for the rest of their lives. His grip on Mara's hand tightened.

She squeezed back. "We'll figure it out," she whispered, her reassurance for his ears alone.

He smiled at her, but didn't share her confidence. "What are we looking for?" he asked, directing the question to Ari.

"I'm not sure. There might be..." Ari stopped, tilting her head as if listening. She turned back the way they'd come. "Oh."

"What?" Mikell quickly turned, searching the endless swirls for any sign of what she'd seen. Nothing. "What is it?" he repeated, looking at her again.

Ari was gone.

He stared at the spot she'd been, then turned around in a slow circle, then another one. Mara looked around, her expression matching the anxiety he felt pounding at the edges of his heart. Had Ari found a way out? If so, how? If not, then where had she gone? He felt a chill and pulled Mara closer.

"She must have figured out how to escape," Mara said. Her words were optimistic, but her voice was thin.

"Right." Mikell didn't quite feel the assurance of his confident nod.

"So there is a way out. We just need to find it." Mara took another slow turn around. She pointed. "She looked that way. We need to go there."

Mikell paused, pointing another direction. "I thought it was this way."

They both looked at the other's chosen direction, then at each other. Mara's eyes searched his, lost and seeking guidance. He had none to give. Instead, he pulled her tightly into his arms. "We'll figure it out. It's going to be okay."

She nodded, then pulled away and straightened. "Let's try this way first."

They walked hand in hand, watching and listening. Mikell wasn't sure how long they'd been walking before the silence became too oppressive. "We should try the other way."

"Are you sure?" Mara looked back over her shoulder. "Which way was it?"

Mikell looked around, though it was a futile action. There was no more distinction in the haze now than there had been before. "I think it was…" He took another look. "I don't know."

Mara looked down. "I'm not sure how we're going to find the way out."

"I'm not either, but I'm not giving up." He tipped her chin to look at him. "And neither are you, raisa-me. We fought side-by-side to take down that entity. Now we'll work side-by-side to escape, no matter what it takes."

Liquid shimmered in the corners of her eyes before she threw her arms around him. "Thank you."

He squeezed back. "Come on. We'll put down my shoe here and use it as a marker. When we decide to change direction, we'll put down another shoe."

She giggled. "And what will we do when we run out of shoes?"

"We'll find something else to…" He felt his cheeks suddenly warm at the implications and gave her a look at her continued giggling. "We'll figure something out, I'm sure." Part of him wanted to be horrified at her impropriety, but another part wanted to join in.

She laughed out loud this time. "I'm sure." She turned, then stopped, tilting her head. "Do you hear that?"

He tilted his head to listen, tightening his grip on her. Ari had vanished after hearing something. "No. What does it sound like?"

There was no answer. He looked down and realized his arms were empty. Mara had disappeared. He spun around, his pounding heart the only sound in the swirling haze. He was alone. "Raisa-me?" he called. "Raisa-me!" Nothing. "Mara!"

He realized that his breath came in sharp jags. It was a struggle to regain control over his chest and even out his breathing. He wouldn't panic. Ari had found the way out. Then Mara. He had to trust that he would, as well. He set out walking, keeping his ears strained to breaking point. They had heard something, he was sure of it. And whatever it was, it held the key of how to escape this green prison.

It felt like he'd walked for ages when he thought he heard something. He came to a complete stop, slowing his breathing and trying to mute the sound of his pulse through his ears. It was as if there was a voice just beyond what he could hear. Or perhaps it was his imagination, his brain driving him mad from the silence and isolation. He wouldn't be surprised by either option at this point.

But it came again, louder. He was sure it was a voice, but could barely hear it, much less tell what it was saying. "Hello?" he called, squinting in the direction he thought the sound came from.

Louder this time, enough he could make out the word. "Mikell." It was Mara's voice.

He bolted toward the sound. "Raisa-me! I'm here!"

"Mikell, I'm here. Listen to me."

"What do I do?" He searched the haze ahead as he ran, but saw no sign of her, or an exit, or any indication of what he should do.

"You can do this. I'm here."

"Do what? How do I get out?" Frustration bit his words. "Mara, answer me!"

"Mikell, please listen."

"I am!" He strained after the sound of her voice with everything he had. "You have to tell me how to get out!"

"Mikell!"

The green haze blurred around him in a sudden hurricane of madness. Then Mara was looking down at him, Ari and Korent hovering over her shoulders. Lut peered at him from the other side, one finger raised as if preparing to poke.

Ari smiled in satisfaction and leaned back. "There we are."

"How do I get out?" he demanded again before full realization returned. He was out. He sucked in a deep breath of relief, feeling his muscles relax.

Mara leaned down and kissed him. "I knew you would find us."

He had no idea how it had happened, but he wasn't inclined to ask. Ari would just talk more nonsense about him being a magic user. As full awareness returned, he realized that he was lying on the cave floor, rocks digging uncomfortably into his back and legs, and head resting on Mara's lap. He still held the stone in his hands. His first instinct was to throw it against the wall, but he stopped, staring. It looked a paler shade of green now, and it was strangely lighter in all other ways, as well.

Ari took it from him. "The entity is gone. We destroyed it."

"So it isn't dangerous to use anymore?" Mara asked.

"I believe that to be the case." Ari wrapped a cloth around the stone. "But I think we might allow Tashan to examine it before taking any chances."

"Agreed," Mikell said, working to sit up. He realized they were still surrounded by Hranites. Most of them snored. Several drooled.

"If we're all in walking shape, then I advise we move on," Korent said, also eying the slumbering enemy with a mixture of amusement, distaste, and caution. "Do we know if they'll be asleep much longer?"

"No way to know for sure," Ari said, depositing the cloth-wrapped stone in her pack. "I'd rather not find out either way."

Korent helped Mikell regain his feet. "Still alive, brother?"

"Probably."

"Good."

Lut skittered ahead of them down the tunnel. The route from there followed a single trail onward, climbing gradually higher and growing lighter and less rocky until they were blinking at approaching sunlight.

"We made it!" Mara all but skipped forward.

Mikell couldn't blame her; his own heart was skipping at the sight of the exit. He hadn't fully realized how oppressive the constant dark and containment of the cave system had grown until the approaching light dispelled the weight of it from his shoulders.

They stepped out into a peaceful grove of ferns, trees, and tall grass. "Of course this couldn't have been the way in," Korent drawled. "Far better to climb around the rocky cliffs."

Ari shook her head, but smiled. "Perhaps this entrance didn't exist when the stone was hidden."

Mara spun around in the dappled sunlight, soaking it in. She looked beautiful, even with grime and dried blood streaking her skin and clothes. Mikell caught her mid-spin and took her through a few more twirls with him, and she laughed in delight as she threw her arms around him.

She paused then, drawing back, and he followed her gaze to see Lut hovering just inside the tunnel. Mara walked over and hugged the underdweller. "Thank you for everything."

Lut shrugged a few times and did his funny dance, then stopped and seemed to pull himself at an awkwardly stiff angle.

Mikell frowned, trying to figure out what the stance meant. It didn't look like how Lut behaved when a threat was approaching, but in anyone else, he would have thought it to be the case. The underdweller held himself stiffly a moment longer, then folded in a deep-angled bow toward Mikell.

Mara burst out laughing and covered her mouth with both hands, her eyes still crinkling with her muted amusement. Mikell tried to fight the smile that tugged at his own mouth and failed. He shook off the humor and returned the stiff bow.

Lut hissed in laughter and danced once more.

Mikell shook his head, still smiling. "We best find our way to move on," he said, turning toward the others. "The sooner we can get back..." He stopped, staring, caught fully off-guard by the sight of Korent and Ari locked in a passionate kiss. He shifted his weight. "Oh. Well." They didn't seem to have noticed he was talking. "Whenever you two are ready..."

Mara pulled him back toward her, one hand gently shifting his attention to her face. "I'm sure we can wait." She paused, a mischievous sparkle in her eye. "And I'm sure we can find some way to enjoy the moment."

The laugh came freely this time as he leaned down to kiss her.

Chapter 19

"Hold still," Mara scolded as she worked the wide comb through Ari's untamable curls.

"I am holding still," Ari muttered, but stopped fidgeting. "Is this going to take much longer?"

"Hopefully not, given that we can't keep everyone waiting." Mara grunted as she struggled to get the comb through a particularly thick mass. "This would be easier if there was some way to just whoosh some magic through it and make it all go in place."

An abrupt wind shot through Ari's hair, whipping it out of Mara's grip and twisting it smoothly together. Ari yelped in surprise. It finished in an arrangement that actually made the mass look tidy and deliberate.

"Huh," Tashan said as she continued into the room, lowering her hand. "I can't believe I never thought of doing that before now."

Ari cautiously reached upward and patted around the edges of her styled hair. "It really worked?"

"I do believe so." Tashan walked slowly around her cousin, inspecting the work. "Aside from here," she said, touching a lock that hung artistically behind the Kadrian's ear, "where it turned purple."

"What?" Ari squawked, grabbing at the hair and pulling it forward to see. When she saw nothing but her usual red, she stuck her tongue out at Tashan. "Brat."

"It looks perfect," Mara said, happy to put the comb aside. She helped Ari to her feet. "We still have the dress to put on."

"Here," Tashan said, picking up the ivory gown, a simple floor-length sheath with wide ties trailing from each side.

Ari eyed it, her lips turned in distaste. "I'm going to look ridiculous."

"You're going to look beautiful," Mara corrected her friend. She and Tashan helped Ari into the dress, working together under Mara's direction to get the ties wrapped in the proper arrangement, crossing the bodice, folding around the waist, and slipping down the back with only a short length remaining to trail on the floor behind Ari. Mara added a touch of kohl to Ari's eyes. "Done."

Ari's expression held a touch of dread as she turned to the mirror. She stared at her reflection in a lengthy silence.

"You look gorgeous." Tashan wrapped an arm through Ari's, then paused, taking on a mock-serious tone. "Why don't you dress like this all the time?"

Ari gave her a look. "I can hurt you."

Tashan suppressed a laugh, her eyes twinkling in amusement.

Ari sighed and looked at the mirror again, lightly toying with one of the face-framing locks of hair. "He's not even going to recognize me."

"Don't be ridiculous." Mara checked outside the balcony door. The room was positioned just above the Meeting Hall's courtyard, a lovely garden filled with the smell of flowers and fruit trees. People sat on the grass below, clustered around a large tree awash in tiny white blossoms where the ceremony would take place.

She glanced at the opposite balcony. Korent grinned at her and gave her a thumbs up. Mikell stood behind him, tugging at his formal belt.

"They're ready," Mara said, returning her attention to the room behind her. "Are you?"

"Tell me why I'm doing this."

Mara smiled. "Because you love him."

Ari rolled her eyes. "No, tell me why I'm having this gussy froufrou instead of just taking a private exchange."

"Because you want to honor your new husband's culture by going through their wedding ceremony," Tashan reminded her.

"Right." Ari sighed, then drew in a deep breath, squaring her shoulders as if preparing to attack an overwhelming enemy. "Let's go."

Mara followed Ari out onto the balcony and down the stairs, smiling at the oohs and ahhs coming from below. Ari and Korent met at the middle point between their opposing staircases, then walked to the tree. Mara and Mikell walked side-by-side behind them, and Tashan took the rear.

Mara snuck a squeeze to her husband's hand before they parted ways to stand opposite each other, behind their respective participants. She'd been surprised when Ari asked her to be the raisa-help, as she'd expected Tashan to be given the honor. But it only made sense that Ari would have her cousin oversee the ceremony instead, leaving Mara and Mikell to take on the roles of raisa-help and tabe-help together.

The ceremony was simple, for all the fuss Ari made over it, and Mara could tell that Ari didn't mind it nearly as much as she'd made it seem. Ari and Korent spoke the traditional greetings and promises, then Mara and Mikell wove a silky ribbon around the pair's hands, metaphorically binding them together. Tashan spoke a blessing, and the ceremony was done with only one thing remaining to complete the tradition: dancing.

The guests cleared space, and music filled the air as Ari paired with an unsurprisingly stiff Mikell and Korent paired with Mara.

"Best day," Korent grinned as he led Mara through the opening steps.

"Isn't she gorgeous?" Mara sighed. "She was afraid you wouldn't recognize her with all the fancying we did."

Korent stole a glance at his new bride. "That's silly. She always looks like that."

Mara couldn't have held back her beaming smile if she'd tried. She leaned in and gave Korent a peck on the cheek. "I couldn't be happier for the both of you." The music swelled, and she followed the traditional steps, shifting back from the center and guiding Korent forward into it as Mikell did the same from the other side, leaving Korent and Ari facing each other in the middle. Mara saw the joy in Ari's eyes and knew there would be no further complaints about the 'gussy froufrou.'

Mikell joined Mara after the newlyweds started in on their first dance as husband and wife. He took her hands and guided her into the dance as other couples joined in around them. "You look lovely."

"Thank you. You look…" She glanced down at his improperly tied belt. "You look great. Handsome as always."

"I tied it wrong."

"Not too badly. It doesn't show." He raised an eyebrow, and she amended, "Not by much."

He glanced over where Korent and Ari twirled together. The Kadrian had always seemed to have a dancer's grace, and it showed more than ever here as she moved fluidly through each step, the trailing ties on her dress swirling around her. "They're a good match."

"Even if she's an outgoing, outspoken magic user?" Mara teased. Her words abruptly came back to her. She still didn't feel like she had changed, but she knew she must have. She'd become more outspoken and interested in magic than she'd once been, and she knew how hard it was for Mikell. "I mean…"

Mikell looked deep in her eyes. "Even if."

She grinned and pulled him close into a passionate kiss.

The End

Pronunciation Guide and Glossary

Alita (uh-LEE-tuh)
Ari (uh-R*EE) [*the *R* is heavily flipped]
Corret (KOH-r't)
Kedlir (KEHD-leer)
Kiven (KEYE-v'n)
Korent (koh-REHNT)
Losanna (l'-SAW-nuh)
Mara (MAH-ruh)
Mikell (m'-KEHL)
Mundin (MUHN-d'n)
Princess Tashan (TAW-sh'n)
Rivon (REE-vawn)
Teylan (tay-LAWN)

Birrik: A medium fern with large fronds that curl toward sunlight throughout the day.

Bramblebuck (BRAAM-b'l-buhk): A bush composed of thorny vines that weave together into a ball shape.

Bristlak (BRIHST-laak): A large, bushy plant known for dense branches and succulent leaves.

Chitling (CHIHT-l'ng): A common Hranite term for an infant denoting uselessness.

Dufo (doo-FOH): A dangerous wild animal with spheroid bodies, long legs, and lengthy, serpentine necks. They exist in family packs, mostly living alone but always within hearing range of at least two other members of the pack. They attack any perceived threat with a sharp beak, talons at the end of their legs, and a foot spike coming from the back of the foot.

Ebrun (EE-bruhn): The western country on Endonsha's landmass, almost entirely inhabited by Hranites.

Elf (EHLF): One of the four races of Kenara, a short people group with large, single color eyes, small noses, and ears featuring a pointed tip.

Emsha (EHM-shuh): The second-largest city in Kenara, a major trade center surrounded by towering walls, founded and predominantly peopled by Elves.

Endonsha (ehn-DAWN-shuh): A planet with a single landmass covering two-thirds of the surface. This landmass is divided evenly into two countries, Kenara and Ebrun.

Hisser Snake: A small, venomous snake that makes its den in dense grasses. It is non-aggressive unless threatened.

Hranite (RAHN-ai't): The predominant race inhabiting Ebrun, a tall people group with vertical eyes, round heads with narrow jaws, no hair, and gray-toned skin.

Innsbrooke (IHNS-br'k): The capital city of Kenara, also the largest city of the land. It is nearly centered beside the wall separating Kenara from Ebrun and has a large lake on the wall side, with two rivers at the north and south end of the city.

Kadrian (KAY-dree-'n): One of the four races of Kenara, a tall people group with high, almost pyramid-shaped pointed ears, flat noses, and wide eyes featuring a vertical slit of a pupil.

Kenara (kehn-AHR-uh): The eastern country on Endonsha's landmass.

Lifsi (LIHF-see): A major city along the main road east of Emsha.

Lutri (LOO-tree): A slender, white tree frequently found in grassland areas of Endonsha.

Markur (mahr-KOOR): The middle ranking of the Kenaran military structure.

-me (MAY): The Elf honorific suffix indicating a deep and romantic love.

Munk (MUHNK): A small bird known for foolish, frivolous behaviors.

Nim (NIHM): One of the four races of Kenara, a people group with particularly lanky limbs, sloping foreheads, and protruding but curveless noses.

Pede (PEED): Small but lengthy insects with numerous legs and a hardened, armor-like carapace.

Raisa (RAY-suh): The Elf honorific for women.

-ro (ROH): The Elf honorific suffix indicating particular respect and honor.

Sentinal (SEHN-tihn-'l): Mount animals, somewhat rare but speedy due to their massive size. They have long, slender legs which stretch above the treetops, round bodies, stretched, snaking necks, and a nose like an upright spear set on a round head.

Sessen (SEH-s'n): A traditional Elf celebration in which a couple marks their first wedding anniversary with a special trip or vacation together.

Slipgrub (SLIHP-gruhb): An especially slimy invertebrate that nests in trees.

Tabe (TAH-bay): The Elf honorific for men.

Treeape (TREE-ayp): Wild simians with two legs and four arms known for their wild flailing when threatened.

Tree-snit (TREE-sniht): Small rodents with large eyes, furry round bodies, and skinny tails, most commonly found clinging to tree bark of a close color to their fur to hide from predators.

Trongial (TROHN-jee'l): A vaguely equine mammal with a long, narrow mouth filled with sharp teeth, a group of which is known as a clutch. They are prized as speedy mounts, but must be kept under careful control due to their feral instincts.

Tulvan (TUHL-v'n): One of the four races of Kenara, a people group with small, flat noses, high cheekbones, wide-set feline eyes, and high, pyramid-shaped ears. They have abnormally strong reflexes and agility, as well as retractable claws. They are known for being deeply religious and believe the Maker gave them power so they can serve in defense of others.

Veelish (VEE-l'sh): A lanky equine animal with long, soft fur

Wastik (WAH-stihk): A general Kenaran term for insects or pests which are to be exterminated.

Wickernik (WIHK-'r-nihk): A large bush with long, frond-like leaves.

About the Author

I enjoy life with my life-mate and little sprout in the Pacific Northwest. I obtained a degree in Counseling Psychology from Northwest University in Kirkland, WA, which I use to create fully dimensional characters with unique personalities and quirks. In fiction, I'm a huge fan of all things speculative: anything where the rules of reality need not apply. My books include traditional fantasy, space fantasy, post-apocalyptic, and more. When not writing, I can usually be found reading, watching movies, or wasting entirely too much time on the internet. Connect with me at cybishop.com

Read more at www.cybishop.com.